The
ABSOLUTELY TRUE STORY...

HOW I VISITED YELLOWSTONE PARK WITH THE TERRIBLE RUPES

THE
ABSOLUTELY TRUE STORY...
HOW I VISITED YELLOWSTONE PARK WITH THE TERRIBLE RUPES

(no names have been changed to protect the guilty)

WILLO DAVIS ROBERTS

Aladdin Paperbacks

First Aladdin Paperbacks edition 1997

Aladdin Paperbacks
An imprint of Simon & Schuster
Children's Publishing Division
1230 Avenue of the Americas
New York, NY 10020

Also available in an Atheneum Books for Young Readers edition.
The text of this book was set in 12/15 Galliard.
Manufactured in the United States of America

10   9

The Library of Congress has cataloged the hardcover edition as follows:
Roberts, Willo Davis.
The absolutely true story . . . how I visited Yellowstone Park with the
terrible Rupes / Willo Davis Roberts. — 1st ed.
p.   cm.
Summary: What they thought would be a dream vacation turns into a
nightmare for twelve-year-old Lewis and his twin sister, Alison, when they
accompany their irresponsible new neighbors on a trip to Yellowstone Park
and are chased by two mysterious men.
ISBN 0-689-31939-8
[1. Brothers and sisters—Fiction.] 2. Behavior—Fiction. 3. Voyages and
travels—Fiction. 4. Mystery and detective stories.] I. Title.
PZ7.R54465Ab   1994
[Fic]—dc20   94-14436

ISBN 0-689-81464-X (Aladdin pbk.)

THE
ABSOLUTELY TRUE STORY...

HOW I VISITED YELLOWSTONE PARK WITH THE TERRIBLE RUPES

Chapter 1

My mom thought the Rupes were a nice, normal middle-class family. When they moved into Marysville they came to our church, and Mr. Rupe joined the summer bowling league. Dad said he was a welcome addition because he had an average of 182. Mom was pleased because Mrs. Rupe offered to sing in the choir, which Mom directed.

So when our new neighbors asked if I could go with them to Yellowstone National Park, to keep their son Harry company, Mom said, "What a wonderful opportunity for Lewis! Of course we'll let him go!"

If she'd known the Rupes a little better, she might not have been so enthusiastic. My twin sister, Alison, figured out pretty early on that Mrs. Rupe let her kids eat anything they wanted, any time they wanted, and that she smoked kind of carelessly, and that she'd let other people look after her kids if they were willing to do it.

But before the trip, none of us saw much of Mr. Rupe, so we didn't know what he was like. He was a bank president, so I guess he was good at that, but if *I* had known how he drove, I wouldn't have even *looked* in his car, let alone gone off with him for nine whole days.

The Rupes only moved in next door a week after school was out, but I think already Mom was tired of having kids around the house. My best friend, Buddy, had gone to spend a month with his grandparents on a ranch in Texas, so I didn't have anybody to do things with. I was bored, too.

The day the Rupes came my sister woke me up and said, "Lewis, come look!"

"At what?" I asked, reluctant to start another long day with nothing in particular to do.

"Someone's moving in next door," she said. She had her face pressed against the window looking down on them. "There's a big yellow moving van, and they've got kids. There's a rocking horse, and a bike."

"Good for them," I said, not moving.

Both Mom and Alison had been fascinated with the new house ever since they started building it six months ago. There used to be a vacant lot there, where we played ball, and none of the kids wanted another house there instead. But every few days, after the workmen had gone home, Mom and Alison would go over and see what had been done. They liked the floor plan, and the sunken living room—though Dad said he wasn't about to break his neck going down a pair of steps every time he wanted to go in and sit in his recliner and read the paper—and when it was nearly finished, they loved the colors in the carpeting and the wallpaper.

"It's gorgeous," Mom had said. "All that tile in the kitchen and the bathrooms—three of them! I wish it were going to be ours."

"I don't," Dad said. "The mortgage on that baby has to be twice what ours is."

"But it's so spacious, and all that pale gold carpeting—"

"Not too practical with the peanut-butter-and-jelly crowd that drips around our house," Dad pointed out. "And as far as space goes, there'll be plenty of room in *this* place once the kids move out. That's only a few years yet."

I get the feeling that the minute Alison and I turn eighteen, we're out on the street. Sometimes it makes me sort of nervous, though Mom talks about us going to college, so I guess they're going to support us long enough to do that.

Anyway, I didn't really care who was moving in next door, but Alison kept on looking out the window and giving me a blow-by-blow description of their furniture—all new except for a big leather recliner—and each family member as they appeared.

"Oh, Lewis, they've got little kids! The boy looks about four, and the little girl about three. Maybe they'll need a baby-sitter."

"Good," I said. If she had baby-sitting money, she'd probably make me a loan if I needed it.

"Oh, there's the mother. She's tall and quite skinny, and she's got the reddest hair I ever saw! So does the little boy. The little girl is more blond. Oh, hey, there's a boy about our age. He's redheaded, too."

I sat up. "Does he look like a jock or a nerd?"

Alison considered. "It's hard to tell. No glasses like yours, but he's carrying a box marked BOOKS. I guess that was his bike. Oh, the man just took a box out of the truck labeled NINTENDO."

I swung my feet over the edge of the bed. "I wonder if he's got any games I don't have."

"Get dressed," Alison suggested, "and we'll go over and see."

Their name, we found out immediately, was Rupe. They had just moved to Washington State from San Francisco. The older boy's name was Harry, and he was twelve.

"I'm Lewis, and she's Alison," I told him. "We're almost twelve, in August."

He looked first at me, then at my sister.

"Is one of you adopted?"

"No."

"Who's the oldest?"

"I am," I said. "By twelve minutes."

He ran a hand through his spiky red hair. "You're twins?"

"Right."

"You don't dress alike."

"I'd look funny in skirts," I said. And then, because Alison wasn't wearing a skirt, I added, "In pink shorts, too. Mom never dressed us alike, even when we were babies. They wanted us to think of ourselves as individuals, not as part of a set of twins."

"I always thought it would be fun to be a twin," Harry said. He had a scab on his chin, in among the freckles, and he scratched at it. "I could think up lots of tricks to play on people if I was a twin." He looked over at our house. "You got anything to eat over there? I'm starved, and we haven't come to the food stuff yet."

"Sure," Alison said. "We haven't had breakfast yet, either. Come on over." Then she paused and looked hopefully at *his* house. "Are your little brother and sister hungry, too?"

"Nah," Harry said. "They've been eating peanuts since we left the motel where we stayed last night."

So we went back to our house and introduced Harry to Mom, who was busy at the computer. She works at home for an insurance company. She said to eat whatever we wanted. That was pretty safe to say because she only buys stuff she says is nutritious.

So we dug into those huge muffins Mom gets at Costco. I had chocolate, Alison had poppy seed, and Harry had one chocolate and one blueberry bran. We drained a quart of orange juice, and then we went up to check out my Nintendo. I had one game he didn't have, and he said he had a couple I didn't have.

He noticed my bookcase. "You read all that stuff?" he asked.

"Yeah. If you want to trade books to read, we could each get some new ones," I told him.

"I'm not much on reading," Harry said, "except comics."

I sighed. Buddy and I read all the same books. Our folks don't want us to spend money on comics, but they're generous with book money. And going to the library gives us a good excuse to get together and fool around when we want to get out of the house. But I wouldn't see Buddy until the end of July. I'd have to make do with Harry.

He was okay. I showed him where the community pool was. We rode bikes and I showed him around. He had plenty of money—it didn't sound as if he had to do any chores to get it, either—and we went to McDonald's for burgers and shakes several times.

Once they got settled in, we had snacks at his house as well as at mine. My mom's idea of snacks is fruit or peanut butter sandwiches. At his house there was a more satisfying variety. He opened up the cupboard and there were Cheese Curls, and corn chips, and potato chips in about four flavors. There was also a stash of candy bars, and once we opened a big can of tamales and heated them in the microwave.

Mom and Mrs. Rupe didn't exactly get to be bosom buddies, because Mom said she's too busy to sit around having coffee and visiting during the day. But she did send a plate of homemade cookies next door. And a couple of times Mrs. Rupe borrowed something they hadn't unpacked of their own yet. They were friendly when they met, but they didn't meet very often. Mr. Rupe put up a swing set and teeter-totter and slide, and when the little kids were out there, Alison went over and talked to them.

"Push me!" Ariadne requested, so Alison helped entertain them for a while. Mrs. Rupe came out with lemonade for everybody and thanked her.

"It's a help to have them out from under my feet when there's so much to do. Billy, don't pull up those flowers, dear. They'll wilt. Leave them in the ground and we can all enjoy them."

"I want to look at them," Billy said.

"Well, bend over, dear, and look at them while they're still growing," his mother said. "Alison, I need to run to the market. I'll only be gone a few minutes. Would you mind watching Billy and Ariadne so I don't have to take them with me?"

"Sure, I'll be glad to," Alison said, really pleased. I hoped that would mean the Rupes would consider her for baby-sitting jobs later on.

"Better your sister than me," Harry said, draining his glass of lemonade. "Come on, let's go over to your place and have a duel with Nintendo."

That afternoon I had to mow the lawn, front and back. I remembered the old Tom Sawyer story, and I offered to let Harry mow part of it if he wanted to.

He looked at me as if I'd gone nuts. "Mow the lawn?" he echoed. "I never mow the lawn."

I made my voice sympathetic. "Oh, won't your folks let you operate the mower? Mine wouldn't, either, last year, but I'm almost twelve now. It's a neat mower; Dad bought it new this year. It's kind of the first step toward driving a car, you know?"

"Really?" Harry asked. I could see I had the hook in him, so I cranked him in a little. "I have to do the front lawn, out where everybody can see it. My folks are particular. But if you want to try it in the back, where it's kind of out of sight from everybody but the family, I'll give you a turn."

I had him, hook, line, and sinker. "You'll show me how to run it?" Harry asked.

"Sure," I agreed. "It's not that hard once you get the idea."

Alison came along while I was sitting on the back steps eating an apple and Harry had sweat dripping off his nose as he mowed the sunny part in the middle of the yard. She looked at him for a moment, then at me.

"You stinker," she said. "Lewis, you are so *lazy*."

"I'm doing him a favor," I told her. "He never got a chance to mow before."

"Poor old Huck," she said, remembering the story from Tom Sawyer, too. We both laughed. She liked to read the same books I did. Maybe they didn't put Mark Twain stories in comic books.

It didn't hurt Harry to take a turn. His face was kind of pink when he got through, and he was thirsty. "Let's have a can of pop," he suggested when we'd put the mower away.

"We'll have to get it at your house. Mom doesn't buy much pop," I said.

8

"If *my* mom didn't buy pop, there'd be a mutiny," Harry grunted. "Come on, I'll get a bag of chips to go with it and we'll sit in the shade."

By the time the Rupes had been there a week, we were in and out of each other's houses all the time. Us kids, I mean. Harry even brought out a Calvin and Hobbes book, which we read together, and then I read aloud from a new paperback mystery called *Nightmare*.

"Hey, I'll come back tomorrow and you can read some more of it," he said when it was time to go home.

I smiled. Maybe I'd make a reader of Harry yet.

When they asked me to go with them to Yellowstone Park, my jaw dropped open. "You kidding?" I asked.

"No. Mom says I'm a pain if I don't have anybody to do things with. Billy and Ariadne are too little to be any fun. We're going to be gone nine days."

I thought it was a great idea. I wouldn't have to mow the lawn or take out the garbage or be reminded every day to clean up my room. And I wouldn't miss Buddy so much.

"You want to go?" Harry pressed.

"Yeah, sure, if my folks will let me. They're kind of particular about what I do." And with whom, I might have added. They wouldn't let me go bungee jumping with Uncle Neal, nor ride with him when he was racing his boat on Lake Washington. And when some of the guys went on a backpack hike up near the ice caves, they said I could only go if there was an adult along to chaperone. We couldn't get a father to go because it was in the middle of the week, so I had to stay home. Everybody else had a great time.

"It wasn't that we didn't trust you, Lewis," Dad said when I complained. "It's just that you aren't quite old enough to do everything on your own, yet. We want you to be *safe*."

So I wasn't at all sure they'd let me go on a trip with the Rupes, even if both parents were along. I was ecstatic when they agreed to let me go to Yellowstone.

Alison was wistful. "It sounds like a wonderful trip," she said.

"I'll bring you a souvenir," I promised. "And send you some postcards, like with a picture of Old Faithful."

That afternoon, two days before we were going to leave, Harry and I were at the Rupes' kitchen table having big bowls of ice cream with chocolate syrup, when his mom came home from the store. She started unloading stuff on the counters—more chips, dip mix, canned pop, cookies, and all kinds of lunch meat.

"Good news," she said to Harry. "Your father decided to make this a really great vacation, so we're renting a motorhome. How about that?"

"Wow! My sister will really be jealous!" I said. "She's hoping maybe you'll need a baby-sitter once in a while," I added, feeling guilty. "But I suppose Harry can do that for you."

Harry shot me a look across the table that should

have shriveled me up like a prune. "Not me! Not with Billy and Ariadne!"

Mrs. Rupe paused with a jar of olives in her hand. "Your sister really likes children, doesn't she?"

"Yeah. Especially babies, but any little kids. She reads to them, plays games with them, things like that."

"She's twelve, did you say?"

"Almost. Same as me."

"Hmm." Mrs. Rupe seemed to find that interesting. She gave me a big smile. "How'd you boys like some chopped walnuts on your ice cream?"

Boy, she sure bought lots of good stuff to eat, I thought. I wished my mom wasn't quite so health conscious. The Rupes even had white bread and Twinkies.

"I think I'll run over and speak to Mrs. Dodge for a moment. Your mother *is* home, isn't she, Lewis?"

"Sure. She's working on the computer," I told her. I knew Mom wouldn't like being interrupted, nor Mrs. Rupe smoking in our house, but just once couldn't be too bad.

So when I got home, Alison met me at the door, all excited. "Lewis, guess what! I'm going to Yellowstone, too!"

"No kidding," I said. "That's great. How come?"

"Mrs. Rupe talked to Mom and said it sure would be wonderful if I went along to help with the little kids. And Mom said she didn't see why not, so now I have to pack!"

"Are you getting paid to baby-sit?" I asked.

"She didn't say anything about paying me. But I'll get to see Yellowstone, and do everything the rest of you are doing. I wonder if my yellow shorts are clean?"

She dashed off to start filling up her suitcase.

I was glad she was going, too. We're pretty good friends, and she's usually good for a loan. I couldn't wait to get started.

"We leave when Dad gets off work on Friday," Harry told me that evening. "This is going to be fun!"

"Yeah," I agreed enthusiastically.

Talk about famous last words.

Chapter 2

On Thursday afternoon the guy from the rental place delivered the motorhome to the Rupe house.

Harry and I were in our backyard, eating cherries off our tree and seeing who could spit the pits the farthest. "There it is!" Harry shouted, and we scrambled down out of the tree and raced for his driveway.

The driver was handing over the keys to Mrs. Rupe. "You have any experience driving a big rig like this, ma'am?" he asked her.

Mrs. Rupe flicked the ashes off her cigarette and they almost landed on Ariadne's head. She didn't seem to notice. "Oh no," she said. "My husband will do all the driving. He can drive anything."

"Okay. All the papers are in order. Your husband already signed them. I just need your signature here, too. Have a good trip," the driver said.

He went out to the car that was waiting for him, and we all swarmed over the motorhome.

It was the biggest one I'd ever seen. On the outside it was cream colored with light blue trim. On the inside it had blue carpeting and upholstery, and it sure was fancy.

"Wow!" Harry said, plumping down in the driver's seat. "I bet they don't have any more·gauges and stuff than this in a 707."

Billy pushed between us to stab at a red button beside a tiny TV on the dashboard. "What's this?" he demanded.

"It's a closed-circuit television," I said. I'd never seen one before, but that had to be what it was; the screen had lit up and I could see Alison coming toward us from the rear. "Neat."

Alison disappeared from the screen and a minute later stuck her head in at the doorway. "Gosh, is this what we're going to Yellowstone in?"

"This is it," Mrs. Rupe said. She still had the cigarette in her hand, though she'd forgotten to smoke it. About two inches of ash fell off it onto the blue carpet. "Dad and I will take the bedroom, you boys can open up the couch, Alison and Ariadne can have the bed that makes up in the dinette, and Billy can have a sleeping bag on the floor."

"I want a sleeping bag," Ariadne said.

"Yes, we'll all use sleeping bags. Only yours will be on a nice bed," Mrs. Rupe said. "Oh, good, there's an ice maker. And look at the size of the refrigerator and freezer!"

"We can take lots of ice cream," Harry said, swiveling in his seat. "Hey, there's a VCR and a big TV, too! Can we rent some new tapes?"

We prowled through the enormous thing, exclaiming over the microwave and the stove and the cupboards and the bathroom with a shower and everything.

"My grandpa has a camper, but it's nothing like this," I said. "I'll bet even Mom would enjoy camping in this, Alison. She says she won't go anywhere there's no bathroom," I explained to Harry. "She wants indoor plumbing and hot water."

"And no bugs," Alison added.

Billy shoved himself between Alison and his mother to examine the toilet. "There's no way to flush it," he said.

"Try the lever there on the floor," I suggested. "Step on it."

Billy put out a foot and stepped on it. Water gushed around inside the bowl, and his face lit up. "Hey, look! It works!"

He just kept standing there, pushing on the lever, while the rest of us moved on to the bedroom at the back of the coach.

It had a queen-size bed, a big closet with mirrored doors, and another TV, this time a little one mounted on the wall.

"Hey, all right!" Harry approved. "We'll get a supply of tapes and watch movies on the way!"

"I wanna watch cartoons," Ariadne said.

"*Star Trek*," Billy said from the bathroom where he

was still watching the water swirl around in the toilet bowl.

"Very nice," Mrs. Rupe said. "All the comforts of home." She took a drag on the cigarette, and scattered ashes across the bedspread before she turned to leave. "Now, everybody get your luggage, and I'll round up the groceries, and we'll start loading up. There are great big storage compartments underneath for whatever we can't get inside."

I'd felt kind of jealous when Buddy left for Texas, but when I told him about taking a trip in this thing, he was going to be absolutely *green*.

Mom and Dad listened to everything Alison and I had to say about the rented motorhome while we ate scalloped potatoes with ham. I took small helpings of the green beans and carrot salad because if I didn't Dad would tell me to anyway.

"Sounds pretty nice," Dad admitted.

Mom sighed. "Wouldn't it be fun to take a trip like that? You kids are lucky to have made friends with the Rupes. You will remember your manners, I hope. Eat whatever they offer you."

"They're going to offer us lots of good stuff," I reassured them. "I saw what they were loading into the cupboards and the refrigerator."

"And do your share of the work," Dad advised. "Pick up after yourselves. Don't expect someone else to do it. Take your turns washing dishes—"

"They're taking tons of paper plates," Alison interrupted.

"And don't interrupt when someone else is talking," Dad continued, but he grinned. "Sounds like it'll be fantastic."

"Honey," Mom said, "do you think we could ever take a trip like this?"

"I don't know if I want to tackle driving something thirty-seven feet long," Dad told her. "I think you almost need to be a truck driver to handle it. A smaller rig might work, though. Where would you want to go?"

"Disneyland," Alison and I said together.

"I was thinking more of a week on the beach," Mom said. "Lying in the sun, listening to the ocean, reading. Eating out."

"The whole purpose of having an RV with a complete kitchen," Dad pointed out, "is so you can save money by doing your own cooking."

"This is my daydream," Mom said, "and it has no cooking in it."

"We'll do everything right," Alison assured them. "So they'll invite us again sometime. And maybe I'll do so well with Ariadne and Billy that they'll want me all summer for a baby-sitter. I have the impression that they drive Mrs. Rupe crazy, and if she has a choice, she'll get a sitter so she can read instead of watching them."

I wondered if, when we came home from Yellowstone, I would still be able to make Harry think it was a treat to run the lawn mower.

We had an early lunch on Friday so we could leave as soon as Mr. Rupe got home. He took off at two o'clock and was home by a quarter after. He was a tall man, the only one in his family with no red in his hair. In fact, he had so little hair, just a fringe above his ears and across the back, that it was hard to see just what color it was. He had freckles, though, like Harry's, all over his arms and hands.

He looked at all the stuff assembled on the lawn and rested his hands on his hips. "You really think this is going to all fit, Ada?" he asked his wife. "Surely we don't need to take everything we own. We're only going to be gone nine days, and they have Laundromats in the campgrounds. And it won't hurt the kids to wear a pair of jeans several days in a row."

Mrs. Rupe was carrying a box of groceries, stuff she'd bought at the last minute. "If you think I'm going on vacation to spend my time in the Laundromat, you're mistaken, Milton. With all that storage space, it will fit if you work at it, I'm sure."

Mr. Rupe worked at it. Twice he had almost everything in, then took it out and started over. Finally it all fit except for some bottled water in plastic jugs that had to sit inside on the floor near the dinette.

"Never know what kind of water you're going to get in strange places," Mrs. Rupe said.

A minute later, Billy tripped over one of the jugs and knocked it into the stairwell, where the cover popped off. The gallon of spring water flooded the steps.

"Well, open the door, Harry, and let it run out," his mother said, so Harry did.

"Are we ready?" Mrs. Rupe asked as the last compartment door was locked and Mr. Rupe joined the rest of us inside. "What's that?"

"That" was someone frantically honking a horn behind us on the street. I put my face against the window to peer out. "It's somebody in another motorhome," I said. "It looks just like this one."

"Idiots," Mrs. Rupe said. "What are they doing, delivering us *two* motorhomes?"

Mr. and Mrs. Rupe got out, so we all did, too. Alison hung on to Ariadne, but Billy raced toward the other motorhome and would have gone right into the street if Harry hadn't grabbed him.

A different guy from the first time got out and walked toward us, smiling. He was kind of heavy and he wore a pair of coveralls that said, ACME V RENTALS, SYD, on the pocket.

"We don't need *another* one," Mrs. Rupe pointed out.

Syd nodded. "I know. But we gave you the wrong one."

A frown was forming on Mr. Rupe's face. "What are you talking about?"

"A new employee didn't know the difference and brought you the wrong coach. I need to trade *that* one for *this* one. The one he brought you by mistake had already been rented to someone else."

The frown got deeper. "What sense does that make, if they're just alike? They *are*, aren't they?"

"Almost, sir. The people who put a deposit on that

one had specified they needed an ice maker, and the other one doesn't have one."

"But we need the ice maker, too," Mrs. Rupe said, frowning the same as her husband. "We're taking all these kids, and we'll be drinking pop for nine days. Of course we want the one with the ice maker, Milton, and we got this one first. They probably aren't traveling with five kids, and they can make ice in the freezer."

Syd started to lose his smile. "I've got the papers right here, ma'am. See? Here's the license number of *that* coach, and the papers are made out in the name of Mr. and Mrs. Carl Hobard. So I have to trade motor-homes."

"That's outrageous!" Mrs. Rupe exclaimed. "Don't let him get away with that, Milton!"

Her husband gave her an annoyed look, but he was even more annoyed with the guy from the RV rentals place. "Do you have any idea how long it took me to pack all that stuff in this coach? If you think I'm going to unload it now, and move it all over again into *that* coach, you're out of your mind."

"But sir, it was a mistake on the part of a new employee—"

"It was a mistake on somebody's part, maybe," Mr. Rupe said, "but it wasn't *my* mistake, and I'm taking the coach I already have. Ada, get the kids back inside. We're leaving."

"But sir—look, Mr. Rupe, it's imperative that we exchange coaches—"

"Not to me, it isn't. If you have a new employee,

someone with experience should be checking on him *before* a customer puts nine days' worth of supplies into a rig. Get in, kids, we're leaving. We're late enough now."

So we got in, and Mr. Rupe closed the door in the guy's face, and took his seat up front.

We were ready to roll. Mr. Rupe turned on the engine, and the big coach throbbed gently beneath us. Mrs. Rupe tightened her seat belt in the copilot's seat up front, and all us kids sat on the couch or the easy chairs or on the floor. We didn't have any seat belts.

Harry leaned back with his hands behind his head. "This is the life," he said.

"Right, this is the life," I echoed. I could see Syd still standing on the lawn, and he looked furious.

Mr. Rupe shifted into reverse and began to back out into the street.

There was a screeching of brakes and then a horn blew furiously. Harry and I turned to look out the window.

"I think we almost backed into Mr. Gilligan's pickup," I said. Mr. Gilligan, who lives across the street, was red-faced and angry looking as he drove around the back end of the motorhome.

Mr. Rupe began to ease backward again, and his wife spoke sharply.

"Watch it, you're going to hit—well, it was only a *little* tree. Maybe it'll grow back."

"This thing's so long it's hard to tell how wide I have to swing to get around anything," Mr. Rupe said under his breath.

"I have to go potty," Ariadne said.

"Can't you at least wait until we're out of the driveway?" her mother asked, but Alison said quickly, "I'll take her, Mrs. Rupe."

My sister stood up and fell forward on her face in my lap. Alison is pretty graceful most of the time, and I was surprised.

Billy, who had been sitting on the floor in front of her, looked up with a cherubic smile. "I can tie shoelaces," he said.

Sure enough, he'd tied Alison's laces together in a double knot. I thought maybe his parents would tell him that wasn't a good thing to do, but they didn't pay any attention. Mrs. Rupe was lighting another cigarette, and Mr. Rupe concentrated on steering the big motorhome down our narrow street without hitting any of the parked cars on either side.

"Be careful, Milton, you're going to scrape the . . . well," Mrs. Rupe said as we lurched over the curb going around a corner, "I guess this takes a little getting used to."

We were only a block from home, and I was beginning to get the idea that Mr. Rupe wasn't such a good driver, at least not with a big rig like this. I looked at Alison, who had just come back from the bathroom, and decided she thought so, too.

I spoke under my breath to Harry. "Did your dad ever drive anything this size before?"

"I don't think so," Harry said. "Don't worry. He'll get the hang of it."

"I'm hungry," Billy announced about the time we went up the ramp onto the freeway. "Can I have a candy bar?"

"You know where they are," his mother said without turning around. "Milton, look out!"

A car narrowly missed us as we merged into the traffic on I-5, and once more a horn blared. Mr. Rupe muttered under his breath again. "You'd think they could see a rig as big as this one and go around it," he said.

I don't drive yet—you can't even get a learner's permit in Washington until you're fifteen and a half—but I knew that a vehicle coming onto the freeway was supposed to blend in with the fast traffic already moving, not just drive in front of it.

My mouth felt a little bit dry, so when Harry got up to get some Cokes out of the fridge, I had one, and so did Alison.

"I want some, too," Ariadne said, and Billy piped up, "So do I."

"Not too much for Ariadne this time of day," Mrs. Rupe said, "or she'll wet the bed. Why don't you get some paper cups down, Alison dear, and divide a can between them?"

Just as she got up to do that, we swerved around a truck and it nearly threw Alison off her feet. She grabbed for the back of a chair and clipped her hip on the corner of the table. She showed me the bruise it left later, a dark purple spot.

She didn't say anything, though, just got the cups

and divided a can of pop between the kids. Ariadne looked into hers. "Ice," she said.

"Ice," Billy echoed, holding up his cup.

Alison added ice to both cups. She had no more than sat down when Billy placed his cup on the floor. A moment later, he forgot it was there and knocked it over with his knee, where it poured ice and pop all over my feet.

"Oh, it spilled," Billy said.

Mrs. Rupe looked around. "Alison, dear, there are plenty of paper towels. Clean it up, will you?"

I bent over and began to pick up pieces of ice, putting them back into the empty cup, while my sister got the towels to sop up the mess. It left a dark, wet spot on the blue carpet.

"Man, this is the way to travel," Harry said. "While you're up, Alison, why don't you get us out a package of those barbecue-flavor potato chips?"

Alison hesitated for a moment, expecting Harry's mother to object, but she didn't, so Alison handed over one of the bags of chips. Harry popped it open and passed them around.

So we roared down the freeway, off on our adventure with all the luxuries anyone could ask for. If my feet hadn't felt so soggy and sticky, and Mr. Rupe's driving hadn't made me kind of nervous—though he did better on the straightaway, where all he had to do was steer forward—I would have figured this was going to be one of the all-time great vacations.

Chapter 3

It was a really great campground where we stayed the first night.

There was a heated swimming pool, and a wading pool for the little kids. Alison could even watch them from the bigger pool, so she could swim, too. "Help me, though, Lewis," she said. "I don't think I can trust either one of them. I remember how Mom used to put life jackets on us. I wish Billy and Ariadne had some."

They loved the water, though neither of them could swim. After Billy came racing toward the bigger pool and jumped in, and we had to fish him out, I thought it might be a good idea to teach him some of the basics. I had an uneasy feeling Alison was going to need more help than I'd figured. We showed them how to hold their breaths and put their faces under the water, so they wouldn't be afraid if they fell in accidentally and we weren't there to rescue them, and how to dog-paddle.

It was nearly dark when we came out of the pool and there were lights on throughout the park. Mr. and Mrs. Rupe had set up lawn chairs beside the motorhome. She was smoking, and he was barbecuing hamburgers on a grill. She had put out a bunch of chips and dip and an ice chest of pop, and there was a carton of deli potato salad.

"What's for dessert?" Harry asked as we were finishing off our third burgers. "Ice cream? With chocolate syrup?"

"Get it yourself," Mrs. Rupe said.

I wondered if Mom would relax her nutritional standards on a trip like this. She likes lots of salads and vegetables, and we don't usually get ice cream more than once a week or so. Her idea of dessert is more likely to be a dish of applesauce or fresh berries.

"Pretty good, huh?" Alison asked, grinning over the enormous bowl of rocky road ice cream she had balanced on her knees.

"Not bad," I admitted, grinning back. "It's going to be a great trip."

It wasn't quite so great when we made up the beds. The couch was supposed to sleep two, but the two needed to be smaller than Harry and I were. I was squashed against the wall. We each had a sleeping bag, but they took up too much space if we used them individually, so we spread his on the bottom and mine on the top for a cover. The trouble was that they couldn't be zipped together because they didn't match, so our feet kept sticking out. When you get up in the mountains, it's cold at night, even in the summer. And the top sleeping bag had a tendency to slide off into the aisle every so often. I'd wake up cold and drag it back. Once Harry rolled off the edge and landed up stuck between the couch and the chairs on the other side of the coach. Motorhomes aren't very wide.

Alison had done the same things with her sleeping bag and Ariadne's. It was on the seats of the dinette, though—the table lifted off the top and became part of the bottom—so her feet didn't stick out because they were against the back of the seat. And Ariadne was smaller than Harry.

Billy's sleeping bag was on the floor between the dinette and the kitchen sink.

"Ouch," I heard Alison say when we had finally turned off the light. "She kicks."

At least Harry didn't kick.

I woke up about dawn to find Alison standing at the foot of the couch, straddling Billy's feet. I knew she wasn't up that time of day for nothing.

"What's the matter?" I asked groggily.

"Ariadne must have had too much to drink after all," she said. "She wet the bed. And me. These are the only pajamas I brought."

Harry didn't wet the bed, either. It made me feel guilty to be the lucky one. "Why don't you just put on the clothes you were going to wear in the morning," I suggested. "Are there clean clothes to put on Ariadne?"

"Yes. I've already changed her, but the sleeping bag on the bottom has a wet spot."

"I saw Mrs. Rupe put a stack of towels in the cabinet in the bathroom. Fold one of them to put over the wet spot so you won't feel it, why don't you."

"I'm glad it was *her* sleeping bag, not mine," Alison muttered as she went to get a towel.

I hadn't gone back to sleep yet—Harry flopped over on his stomach and stuck his elbow in my ear just as I started to doze off—when I heard somebody walking around outside.

We were in a campground with about a hundred other rigs, so I knew there were other people close by. But it was early, and I wondered why anybody was so close to our motorhome when the nearest trailer was at least thirty feet away.

I rose and looked out the open window beside me. I could just barely make out a figure in the dim light because the guy was wearing a white shirt. He was sort of sneaking along, right beside our coach.

I tried to remember if Mr. Rupe had left anything outside that somebody might try to steal, but I didn't think so. He'd packed away the folding chairs and all that stuff so we'd be ready to leave right after breakfast.

The guy stopped suddenly, as if he were listening, and for a minute my heart raced, because he seemed to be looking right at me through the window, though I knew he couldn't possibly see me. There was no light inside at all.

Then he moved again, and seconds later I heard

him hit the supporting bar of the awning Mr. Rupe *had* forgotten to retract. It caught him right in the middle of the forehead, and I heard him grunt, and then he swore under his breath.

Across the coach, from the bed on the dinette, Alison said, "What was that?"

The guy outside dropped like a stone. I couldn't see him anymore, but by pushing my face against the screen I caught a glimpse of his shirt as he scuttled away and finally stood up when he got into the nearest trees. Then he disappeared, and I couldn't see where he went.

"Lewis?"

"Some guy who was lost," I guessed. "He whacked his head on the awning support. Swore when it hurt."

"Oh. It does hurt. I did it, too, the first time I walked around that side of the coach. Let's go to sleep, Lewis."

"Okay," I muttered, and poked Harry so he'd roll over and get his arm out of my way so I could lie down again.

When we got up, Mrs. Rupe didn't seem surprised that Ariadne had wet the bed. "I was afraid she was drinking too much," she said. "When we get to camp tonight, we'll wash everything. Even the sleeping bag's washable."

At home we usually have cereal and fruit for breakfast, except on Sunday mornings when Dad often makes pancakes or waffles. Mrs. Rupe had brought frozen waffles that we heated in the toaster, and nobody told me not to use so much syrup. Harry and I ate six apiece; they weren't very big.

We had to fold up the couch and stash all the sleeping bags and pillows back in the underneath compartment. That morning we got back on the freeway without running over anything or having anyone honk at us. I hoped that meant Mr. Rupe was getting the hang of driving the big rig.

Harry loaded a tape in the VCR, and we watched a movie on the small TV in the back, all of us kids sprawled on the bed. Ariadne and Billy were intrigued by the way the toilet flushed, so they kept having to go potty. Alison usually went with Ariadne, so she missed parts of the movie, but it was one she'd seen before, so it didn't matter too much.

Every little while Harry would make a foray into the kitchen for refreshments. It wasn't easy to walk around when the coach was moving. If the driver slammed on the brakes or swerved out to pass, you got thrown around if you weren't hanging on well enough.

Billy didn't want to watch the movie, so he climbed off the bed and looked for other entertainment. I guess the rest of us weren't paying too much attention to him, because the next time Alison got up to get something to drink, she discovered he'd emptied all the drawers in the nightstands. Mr. and Mrs. Rupe's underwear was scattered all over the floor.

Alison scolded him a little, and when he refused to pick any of it up, she did it herself, folding it neatly before putting it back in the drawers. She nudged me when she folded the last pair of shorts.

I checked them out. "Cute," I said, as she put them in the drawer. Little red hearts all over them.

"Maybe besides swimming we need to teach them to mind better," Alison said, after looking toward Harry to make sure he was absorbed in the movie. "Like they should pick up the messes they make."

"What do you mean, *we?*" I asked.

My sister gave me a look. "You're not going to desert me, are you, Lewis? I'm not sure I can keep track of these two all by myself."

"Well, okay. You teach them some manners, and I'll teach them to swim," I compromised. "Where's Billy now?"

Alison ducked her head around the corner to look. "Come out of there, Billy. You can't keep flushing the toilet."

"But I want to," Billy responded.

"But you can't," Alison said firmly, and hauled him back into the bedroom by his shirt.

"I'll tell Ma you're being mean to me," Billy threatened mutinously, his lower lip jutting out.

"Not if you want us to take you swimming when we get to the next camp," I said, leaning my face down close to his. "You want me to give you another swimming lesson tonight?"

He thought it over. "Before supper?"

"If there's time. I don't know when we'll get there."

"Okay," Billy said. Suddenly he reached up and grabbed my glasses. "What is this thing?"

I yelped and grabbed them back. "My glasses. I need them to see with, and if you take them off that way, it hurts, okay? I need them on again."

"I want them," Billy said, unwilling to let go.

"You can't have them. Without them I'm too near-sighted to see very far," I told him, prying his fingers off the bow.

"Let him look through them, Lewis," Alison suggested. "Then it will satisfy his curiosity."

So I put them on his little nose and held them in place. He stared at me through them. "You have hairs on your face."

"Hairs? You mean my eyebrows? Everybody has eyebrows. Even you do. See?" I put out a finger and traced his.

He rolled his eyes, trying to see upward. "Show him in the mirror, Lewis," Alison said, so I slid off the bed and took him into the bathroom. There was a full-length mirror in there, and Billy leaned up close to it. First he looked through my glasses, then when I took them off he practically put his nose on the glass and felt his eyebrows.

"Hairs," he said.

"Yeah. Now come on," I said as I settled the glasses into place, "let's go back and watch the rest of the movie."

"I'm hungry," Ariadne said when we returned to the bedroom.

"I'll ask your mother what you can have," Alison said.

"Candy," Ariadne told her.

"I'm not sure about that. It'll be lunchtime soon," Alison warned her, but after she consulted with Mrs. Rupe, she shrugged. "She says they can have anything they want, even candy bars. I brought one for each of the rest of us, too. For all I know, maybe this is lunch."

It wasn't, though. We pulled into a rest stop. Mrs. Rupe said, "Everybody fix your own sandwiches. Alison, dear, you'll fix Billy's and Ariadne's, won't you?"

Outside, a horn tooted. Mr. Rupe had pulled crossways in about five parking spaces, and someone who wanted to use one of them was glaring in our direction.

"What's wrong with him?" Mr. Rupe said. "Can't he see it takes this much space to park a rig this size?"

Harry had his face pressed against a window. "Uh, Dad, I think RVs are supposed to park on the other side, where the trucks are. They have longer parking spaces, and you don't have to back up to pull out of them."

"Oh. Well, I'll do that next time. Is that what that sign means, with the pictures of cars and trucks on it? You'd think they'd put some words, so you could tell what they meant. Ada, make me a couple of pastrami sandwiches, will you? I'm going to get out and stretch my legs for a minute."

It was a jam-up in the kitchen, so Harry and I got

out to walk around, too. A lot of people had stopped to use the restrooms and the picnic tables. Several people gave us dirty looks, and it was sort of embarrassing. Two cars went on through the rest area without finding a place to park, because we were taking up so much space.

A light blue Crown Victoria had taken the last parking slot, right alongside us. There were two people in it, but I didn't pay any attention to them except to wonder why they stopped. They weren't eating, and they didn't get out to use the restrooms.

When we got back in the coach, everybody else was wolfing down sandwiches. We fixed ours, and put plenty of ice in our pop, and Harry opened another bag of chips. I wondered what my mom would think about splitting a big bag every time we wanted a snack. Nobody ever seemed to think Harry was overdoing it. For the first time in my life, I was getting all the snacks I wanted, so I wasn't complaining.

After we gathered up all the trash and carried it out to the garbage can, we were ready to go again.

"Everyone sitting down? Okay, here we go," Mr. Rupe said. "Oh, for heaven's sake, that car is in my way. I'll have to back up to get out. Harry, look and see if I can go straight back without hitting anything."

We checked, and he could, but he didn't back up quite far enough. When he went to pull forward, he came within about an inch of touching the Crown Victoria. I got a glimpse of the driver's horrified face as we skimmed by without actually scraping any of his paint. *Sheesh!* I hoped we'd park on the truck side next time, so he didn't have to go into reverse.

Ariadne wanted to watch cartoons, so Harry and I stayed up front. We were going *down* the mountain, now, into eastern Washington, and instead of all kinds of green trees and little waterfalls everywhere, we got into dryer country. Apple and cherry orchards, mostly, and when we saw a big sign, FRESH CHERRIES, Mrs. Rupe insisted we stop and get some.

They were delicious, and nobody told us how many we could have. We just ate all we wanted. I wondered what it was like to have parents who let you do whatever you wanted. I guessed I'd never know.

We got bored after a while, with no decent scenery to watch after we passed the orchards and got out into naked hills. The grass was all turning brown under the summer sun. I knew it wouldn't be like that at Yellowstone, because we were supposed to see a lot of wild animals there. It didn't look as if even a jackrabbit could survive out here.

The road began to wind down to the level of the Columbia River, far below us. It was a really steep grade. Mrs. Rupe got nervous, and I sort of did, too.

"Milton, we're going awfully fast, aren't we? Slow down! There's another curve coming up!"

"Do you think I don't know there's one curve after another? I know we're going fast, but I don't want to use the brakes *all* the time or they'll get hot and then we won't *have* any brakes!" Mr. Rupe sounded so cross that nobody else said anything for a minute.

And then I could smell it. Hot brakes. Ours, or someone else's?

Most of the other people on the road were in cars, not in a motorhome, and none of them seemed to be having any trouble. Every minute or so we'd catch a glimpse of the river, still quite a long way down.

What if we lost our brakes and couldn't stop at the bottom?

"Uh—" I started to say, and strangled on the words. How can a kid tell a grownup how to do something the kid can't really do?

"What?" Harry asked, and when I looked at him I thought he was getting a little bit scared, too. "You've been over here before, haven't you, Lewis? Didn't you say your grandpa has a camper?"

"Yeah," I said, feeling as if my mouth were full of dry cornflakes, "a little one on his pickup."

"Did you ever go down this steep a grade in it?" Harry demanded, watching the speedometer as we picked up speed.

"Yeah. Grandpa says instead of using the brakes to slow you down on this kind of road, you use . . . uh, the gears. Like you shift into a lower gear and the engine acts to retard your speed, you know?"

"*I* don't know anything about it," Harry said, but raised his voice. "Hey, Dad, shift down and it will keep us from going faster and faster!"

"What do you know about it?" Mr. Rupe said, but his wife reached over and grabbed his arm.

"Milton, for heaven's sake, try it! This is frightening the kids!"

"Oh, for pete's sake," Mr. Rupe said, but to my relief he did shift down. And we could all feel the coach slowing.

I let out the breath I'd been holding when we finally reached the bottom and headed across the bridge at a reasonable speed. And then, when we started to climb up out of the canyon on the other side, we slowed way down. So slow that practically every other car passed us, everybody but the trucks.

"Maybe I should have let them trade us motorhomes," Mr. Rupe said, sounding more frustrated than ever. "This one sure doesn't seem to have much power."

I saw a puff of black smoke up ahead of us. If we came to a complete stop we'd be stuck out here miles from anything, and I'd figured out by now that Harry's dad had probably never driven anything that wasn't completely automatic. Another puff of smoke rose from the 18-wheeler in front of us. "Uh, Mr. Rupe, that truck driver up there is shifting down to climb the grade, just like you did to get a slower speed coming *down*. That's what we need to do, too, I think. My grandpa says you shift down on any grade, whether you're needing the extra power to climb or need the engine to hold you back."

I was afraid he'd tell me to mind my own business, but he was scaring me enough so it might be worth it if he took my suggestion.

"Try it, Milton," Mrs. Rupe urged. "We can't be doing more than ten miles an hour this way."

A car whizzed past us, a light blue Crown Victoria, and I saw a blur as a face looked out at us, and then it surged on ahead and passed the truck, too.

Alison was sitting opposite me, holding Ariadne on her lap, and she looked as tense as I felt. I heard her sigh when without any comment Mr. Rupe tried shifting down. We didn't go any faster, but at least we didn't stop altogether.

"I didn't know any of that stuff about the gears," Harry said. "How come you know? Do they teach you that in driver's ed?"

"I don't know. I'm not sure. I learned about it from my grandpa. He likes explaining things to me when we're together."

"Are we going to make it to the top?" Mrs. Rupe asked anxiously. "I never expected this trip would make me so nervous."

She lit another cigarette and took a long draw on it. Nobody in our family smoked, and the smell of it was starting to make me kind of desperate for some cleaner air.

"They should give you an instruction manual with these things," Mr. Rupe said, and I wondered if he was as nervous as the rest of us. I sure would have been, trying to drive something this big for the first time. Eventually we came to the top, and I let out a long breath.

Ahead were more dry hills. Nothing to look at, so

we went back and watched a Disney animated movie. We took the cherries with us, but that was a mistake.

"Lewis," Alison said after a while, "I think you'd better put the cherries away. Billy's getting juice all over everything, and I'm afraid he'll get sick."

It was a long way to Yellowstone. Even eating and watching movies wasn't enough to keep it from being kind of boring after a few more hours.

"You'll like this next campground," Mrs. Rupe told us when the little kids complained. "It has a petting zoo. Baby animals you can touch, Billy. Billy likes to touch things," she explained to us.

Alison and I refrained from saying we'd noticed.

"I want to swim," Ariadne announced.

"You can swim, too. When I made the reservations I chose all the places with heated pools. Sit down, Billy, or you'll fall."

Right then Billy lost his footing and slammed into Harry's lap, spilling the box of cherries he'd managed to get hold of again after Alison had taken them away.

We all scrambled around, picking up cherries and trying not to squash them. Somehow just the sight of them made me feel queasy.

The campground was all we'd been promised, though. We swam first, and I took time to give Billy a lesson. He caught on pretty quick. Ariadne learned how to open her eyes underwater, and she was all excited about it.

Then we walked over to the petting zoo. Billy was enchanted with the baby miniature goats, and even

Harry and I thought they were pretty cute. They stuck their heads through the fence so you could rub them. There were llamas, too, and donkeys, with a baby one that made a sound like a squeaky gate, and a baby miniature horse that was smaller than lots of dogs, and all kinds of peacocks and ducks and geese that would come running for the food you could buy for them.

"Let's go see if supper is ready yet," Harry said finally, and we headed back toward our campsite.

We could smell hamburgers and chicken and steaks cooking all around us. I was beginning to feel hungry after all.

And then I saw the light blue Crown Victoria again. It was almost hidden under the trees, but I was pretty sure it was the same one.

"Funny," I said to Alison. "You'd think people traveling in a car would go to a motel, not a campground."

She wasn't paying any attention. "Ariadne, don't get too close to that dog, it might bite!" she called. "Billy, we're going *this* way! Lewis, catch him!"

Billy changed directions, laughing, when I started after him. If Harry hadn't cut him off, he probably would have run right into a family roasting hot dogs.

I didn't think any more about the blue car.

Chapter 4

"This was a very stressful day," Mrs. Rupe said. "I sure don't feel like fixing a meal. Let's order in some pizza. They'll deliver out here to the campground. I saw their sign."

So we all pigged out on pepperoni and sausage pizza, washed down with Cokes and grape soda. They were having an ice cream social at the rec hall, so we got in on that, too.

I didn't have seconds, like Harry. Maybe I'd eaten too many cherries earlier.

The rest of the kids wanted to go in the water again, but I didn't feel like doing that, either. I sat on the edge of the pool and gave Billy another dog-paddling lesson. He was doing pretty well. If he fell into the water accidentally, he'd probably be able to keep himself afloat without panicking.

The pool was across the road from the office,

where there were a pair of pay phones. Dad had said to check in with them at home and let them know how we were doing. Just about the time I got ready to go call, though, I saw that both phones were busy.

One of them was being used by a lady in a big hat with a little dog under one arm. I stared at the guy at the other one.

He seemed familiar, somehow. I couldn't think why. Kind of short and stocky, going bald on top. He waved one arm while he talked, and then he hung up as if he were annoyed. He went into the combination office/store when he was finished, so I told Alison I was leaving Billy and went to call.

I talked to Dad for about five minutes. It was hard, in a way, because I didn't want to admit that Mr. Rupe was having trouble with the motorhome. If I had, Dad would have jumped into the car and come after us. So I talked about the campgrounds and pools and the petting zoo. And when Mom came on and asked if we were eating right, I said, "Oh, sure, we're eating whatever they serve, and it's been great. We have one more day of riding, I guess, before we get to the camp outside of Yellowstone, and then the next day we go into the park."

"How's Alison doing with the baby-sitting?"

"You know Alison. She's real good with kids," I evaded. I didn't mention that she seemed to have wound up taking full charge of these two.

"Well, have fun," Mom said. "Tell Alison we miss you both."

Alison had the kids out of the pool by the time I got back, and Harry said he'd had enough, too. We cut through the campground on the way back to our site, and we went past that blue car I'd noticed several times. I suppose because I watch too many cop movies, I glanced at the license plate. Washington number AVA 703.

It seemed funny, a nice car like that sitting there with no trailer or anything. They hadn't even put up a tent the way some of their neighbors had.

A few spaces down some college guys were spreading out sleeping bags on the ground and eating off the back of their van. Maybe the people in the blue car had sleeping bags.

As we went past the blue Crown Victoria, the man who'd made the phone call just ahead of me came up and got into the car. I got a good look at the guy. Maybe the only reason he looked familiar was that I'd seen him looking at us when they passed us earlier that day, I reasoned.

We all changed out of our swimsuits and walked over to the playground. The little kids climbed on all the equipment and made a lot of racket while Alison kept them from killing themselves. Harry and I played catch for a while, until his mother called him.

"Harry, run over to the store and get me some cough drops," she said.

Harry grimaced. "Okay. Come on, Lewis."

I threw an uneasy glance at my sister. One of her charges was on a swing, the other one at the top of the slide, and I knew how fast each of them could run—in opposite directions.

"Uh, I think I'd better stick around here and help Alison ride herd on the little kids," I said.

He shrugged. "I'll be back in a few minutes, then."

It was a good thing I stayed. Before Harry had gone twenty feet Ariadne fell out of the swing and scraped her knees. While Alison was picking her up, Billy came down the slide head first and could have cracked his skull if I hadn't been there to catch him.

"What a pair," Alison groaned, after convincing Ariadne that she didn't need Band-Aids. "Let's sit down outside the motorhome and we'll read a story. I brought a book with lots of good pictures to share with you."

"Don't want a story," Ariadne said. "I'm hungry."

"Me, too," Billy chimed in. "Let's go have some ice cream."

I didn't see how either of them could eat any more ice cream, but by this time I knew their eating habits were different from ours. "It's all gone," I told them. I was beginning to wonder how I wound up spending my fabulous vacation being as much a baby-sitter as my sister was.

Billy smiled at me. "We'll buy some more," he said.

"Sorry," I told him. "Neither of us has any money." We *did* have some in our suitcases, but I didn't intend to use any of it for ice cream for these kids whose parents could—and usually did—buy them anything they wanted.

"I've got money," Billy said proudly. "See?"

He reached in his pocket and drew out a bill. When I got a good look at it, I choked.

"Where'd you get that?" I demanded.

"Found it," Billy stated. "Finders keepers, right?"

He let me take the bill out of his hand, and I extended it to Alison. "Look at this. I never saw a hundred-dollar bill before."

She bit her lower lip. "Where did you find it, Billy? Whoever lost it probably needs it. It's a lot of money."

"We can buy a lot of ice cream," Billy affirmed. "I want chocolate, and Ariadne can have strawberry."

Alison's eyes met mine, then focused on the little boy. "Billy, I think we have to find the person this belongs to and give it back. If it were only a dollar, it might not matter so much. But it's a lot of money. Where exactly did you find it?"

"I don't know," Billy said.

I didn't know whether to believe him or not.

"I want strawberry ice cream," Ariadne put in.

Billy reached up and took back the bill before I tightened my hold on it. "It's mine," he said. "When you find something, it's yours. Dad says."

"Not always," Alison told him, troubled. "Little things, maybe, but this is too much. Someone may be looking for it because they really need it. Did you find it by the swimming pool?"

He hesitated, then shook his head. "No."

"Where, then? Here in the playground? No? By the motorhome?"

Billy hesitated. "Maybe."

"Maybe where? By the motorhome?"

"On the ground?" I asked.

"No," he said, and then, "I don't remember."

That was the best we could get out of him. When Harry came back with his mom's cough drops, we told him about the money.

"A hundred bucks? Hey, show us where you got it, Billy! Maybe there's some more in the same place."

He was treating it like a joke, which made Alison and me uncomfortable. I wasn't sure what to do, and I said so.

"What's the big deal?" Harry asked. "Somebody lost it, Billy found it. Unless the guy comes looking for it, it's Billy's, right?"

"How's the owner going to know where to look? Or whom to ask?" Alison wanted to know.

"That's his problem." Harry shrugged it off. "You know, it could be changed into a lot of quarters. We could go over to the game room and play video games all night."

"It's mine," Billy declared firmly. "I want ice cream."

And then we forgot about the money because something exploded with a heck of a noise. When we looked toward the office, we saw smoke pouring out, and people started running in that direction.

We moved along with everybody else, Alison grabbing the little kids by the hands. Even Mr. and Mrs. Rupe got up and tagged along, him carrying a cup of coffee and her with another cigarette smoking in one hand.

"What happened?"

"What's going on?"

"Somebody call the fire department!"

"The store's on fire! There's somebody in there!"

People were yelling and moving around. Dad always told us not to get in the way when there was an emergency, but Harry obviously never got any such instructions. He wanted to push right to the front of the gathering crowd and see what was going on.

"Billy, stay right here with me," Alison said, and made a grab for him, but Billy jerked away from her.

"There's the kitty," he said.

Sure enough, a big gray-striped cat had come bounding out ahead of the people hurrying out of the burning store. It ran right in front of us, and before I could react, Billy was chasing the cat, darting between the legs of those coming to watch.

"Lewis," Alison cried, "catch him! I can't run hanging on to Ariadne!"

I glanced toward where the Rupes were standing, but they weren't paying any attention. Harry had already pressed right up close to the front of the crowd, so he wasn't going to be any help, either.

I wanted to stay and watch, too. There was smoke billowing out of the store, and the manager was choking and gasping, and I could hear the fire engines coming.

Alison gave me a pleading look, and I turned resignedly and started after Billy.

By the time I caught sight of him through the tourists who were leaving their campers and motor-homes to see what the excitement was, he'd barreled into an old lady and nearly knocked her down. I gained on him but couldn't quite reach him yet when the cat changed direction and headed right for our campsite with Billy a foot or so behind.

"Billy! Come back here!" I yelled.

I might as well have saved my breath. Nobody paid any attention to me.

He followed the cat around the back of the motorhome; I plunged after him, and ran smack into somebody pretty solid.

The air went out of both of us.

"Sorry," I muttered, scarcely looking at the man. I made a final grab and caught Billy's shirt.

"I want the kitty!" he bellowed, almost jerking away from me.

"Forget it! It's not your cat, and you can't take off by yourself that way," I told him. By that time the cat had vanished.

Billy turned around and kicked me squarely on the shin, and for a moment I wanted to smack him, but I didn't.

I held on to his shirt, though. "Behave," I said through my teeth.

It wasn't until we were halfway back to where the

fire engines were pulling in that I realized the guy I'd run into by the door of our motor home was the passenger from the blue Crown Victoria. He must have been taking a shortcut through our campsite, I thought.

The fire was kind of an anticlimax. It had started in a dumpster up against the back wall of the store, and they put it out before it did anything but fill the place with smoke.

The fire engines were gone almost before I got a good look at them.

It was too bad, I thought, that the Rupes hadn't put Billy and Ariadne in a kennel or something instead of bringing them along. They weren't really enjoying this trip, just spoiling it for the rest of us.

Of course, if they hadn't been there, Alison wouldn't have come either.

I sighed, hoping they wouldn't be able to spoil Yellowstone itself. I forgot to wonder any further why that oddly familiar tourist in the car without a trailer had been practically by our door when I went chasing Billy back there.

Chapter 5

Harry was roasting marshmallows over the campfire and Alison was helping the little kids with theirs while Mrs. Rupe reclined watching the small portable TV from the bedroom compartment. During a commercial, she smiled at me. "Don't you like marshmallows, Lewis?"

"Uh, yeah, usually," I said uneasily. Just looking at them after all that pizza and ice cream made me queasy. "Not tonight, though."

She looked around. "Where did Milton disappear to?"

"I think he walked over to talk to those people in that mini motorhome," I said, gesturing.

She nodded. "Oh," she said, and then, "did you want something, sir?"

I glanced up, and there he was again. The guy I'd run into while I was chasing Billy.

He smiled. It looked like he had false teeth. "I dropped my car keys earlier today somewhere around here. I wondered if you'd found them."

"No. I didn't see any," Mrs. Rupe said.

Everybody else shrugged or shook their heads. "Nope," Harry said.

The false teeth vanished. "Well, thanks anyway," he said, and went on across the grass.

"Didn't he look kind of familiar?" Mrs. Rupe asked nobody in particular. "Who is he?"

Nobody answered.

"Lewis," my sister said, "would you get me a wet washcloth? I don't dare let go of Ariadne until I've cleaned off her hands. They're pretty sticky."

"I thought you were the baby-sitter," I said, but I got up from the picnic table bench. I knew perfectly well one girl alone couldn't keep up with both those kids.

"Bring me a can of pop on your way back," Harry called, and I flipped him a wave of acknowledgment. How he could still be eating and drinking was beyond me.

I went into the bathroom and got a washcloth, running water over it and then wringing it out. As I started to leave the rig, something clinked against my foot and I looked down.

Keys. About eight of them, on a key ring with a Seattle Seahawks medallion on it.

I bent and picked them up. I hadn't noticed how Mr. Rupe carried his keys, but I hadn't seen anyone else have any, so I took them along, remembering at the last minute to get Harry a can of 7UP, and went back outside.

Harry took the pop without saying "thank you," and Alison did thank me for the washcloth, which she promptly applied to a squirming Ariadne. I extended the keys toward Mrs. Rupe.

"I guess Mr. Rupe dropped these in the bathroom," I said.

She glanced at them, still half-absorbed in her sitcom. "No, those aren't Milton's. He doesn't have a key ring like that. Oh!" For a few seconds she actually looked at me. "That man was looking for keys. Maybe they're his."

"Inside our motorhome?" I asked, incredulous.

"Oh, probably one of the children found them and took them inside. Why don't you go see if you can find him and ask?"

I looked at Billy, who shook his head. "I didn't find them. Can I have that thing? I like the Seahawks."

"No, it belongs to the guy who lost the keys," I said. I hesitated, then glanced at Harry. "Well, okay, I'll take them back to him. You want to come?"

"Sure," Harry said, drinking half his 7UP in one long gulp.

We didn't see the passenger from the Crown Victoria, but the man I guessed to be the driver was sitting at the picnic table beside the car, reading the paper and drinking something out of a paper cup. He looked at us but didn't speak until I held out the keys. "Are these the ones that were lost?"

He gave me a neutral glance, then accepted the keys. "Thanks," he said, and went back to reading his newspaper.

"You're welcome," I said. As we walked away I remarked to Harry, "Friendly fellow, wasn't he? Listen, the other guy was right there by our coach during the fire. What if Billy and Ariadne *didn't* find the keys. What if that guy dropped them inside himself?"

"What would a stranger be doing in our motorhome?" Harry asked. "Nah, Billy probably did it. He just didn't want to admit it."

I didn't see why he'd hesitate to tell the truth. Nobody ever punished or even scolded him no matter what he did. But I didn't say anything.

The next day we got out of the campground without running over anything but a hose stretched across the road. Somebody yelled after us, but Mr. Rupe didn't seem to hear him.

"Tomorrow we'll be in Yellowstone," he said as we drove along the highway. "It was the first national park, you know. And it's still the most visited of them all. We'll see all kinds of wild animals and geysers and those mud pot things."

"What are geysers?" Billy asked, and Harry said, "Mud doesn't sound interesting."

"The geysers are hot water that spouts up out of the ground under pressure," I said. "Dad looked it up in the encyclopedia when we knew we were coming. They call the most famous one Old Faithful, because it goes off so often, twenty-one to twenty-three times a day. It squirts as much as one hundred thirty to one hundred eighty feet up in the air, seventy-five hundred gallons a day."

Harry was scowling. "We came all this way to see tons of water and *mud*?"

"It's *boiling* mud," I said. "My dad told us about it. And I think some of it's colored."

"Big deal," Harry said. "I'd rather see all the wild animals."

"Are there tigers?" Billy asked eagerly.

"No tigers," I told him. "Bears, maybe. And deer and elk and moose. And buffalo."

"I want to pet a bear," Ariadne piped up.

Alison shook her head. "These are *wild* animals, Ariadne. You can't pet them. You can only take pictures of them."

The little girl's eyes were wide. "Will wild animals bite me?"

"Not if you stay back away from them," Alison assured her.

"Can we feed them?" Billy asked.

"No. You aren't allowed to feed them," I said, glad Dad had looked up a little about it. "It would make them sick."

Actually, the food *we* were eating was beginning to make *me* sort of sick. Alison and I had never had so much junk food in our lives, and we'd only been gone from home for a few days. I never thought I'd look forward to a salad or a serving of peas, and even broccoli sounded better than another potato chip.

"We're going to stay in a campground outside of Yellowstone," Mrs. Rupe told us. "It's not far away, and it has better facilities than the park," she said. "We'll have a store and a laundry and a playground for the little kids, and an indoor heated pool. Besides, the campgrounds inside the park were all full by the time I called."

The campground turned out to be neat. We went to the swimming pool first thing. It was surprising how fast Billy and Ariadne were catching on to swimming. They weren't especially graceful, but they could keep themselves afloat all right.

Harry was the kind of guy who liked to sneak up behind you and jerk you under. He even did it to Alison, who didn't care for it much when she didn't have a chance to get a good breath of air first. There were some other kids there, though, and they invited us to a water volleyball game with a big ball, and that distracted Harry from any more dunking.

The RV park was full, and after a while so many people came in the pool that we decided to get out. "Hey," Harry said, "let's go play video games. There's an arcade right off the laundry room."

I knew Harry had more spending money than I did, and I wasn't sure how much I wanted to spend on video games, so I was glad when Alison came to call us to supper.

We walked back to our campsite, smelling everybody else's hamburgers and hot dogs being grilled. People were sitting around their picnic tables or eating in their rigs with the doors open, so we could tell what most of them were having. I hadn't eaten any junk all afternoon, so I was hungry. I hoped we weren't having more chips, at least for tonight.

We were, though. With grilled cheese sandwiches. Mr. and Mrs. Rupe had been invited over to the Nabakowskis, in the mini motorhome from the last campground, for steaks.

"You kids can toast your sandwiches all right, can't you?" Mrs. Rupe asked cheerfully. Without waiting for a reply, the Rupes were out the door and gone.

I looked at the refrigerator. "Is there anything green in there?"

"A head of lettuce. There was a cucumber, but I think it got slimy already. Listen, I'll fix hot sandwiches and make a salad if you'll take Billy and Ariadne outside and watch them. I can't do this and keep track of them, too. Make them sit at the picnic bench."

So I tried. Harry could have helped, but he didn't. He was talking to a girl in red shorts from the trailer two spaces down.

I sighed. "Sit right here," I told the little kids, "while I bring out the paper plates and stuff, okay?"

When I came back, fifteen seconds later, Ariadne was gone. Billy was watching a column of ants cross the table to a spot of what might have been jam left by the last users.

"Where's your sister?" I demanded.

Billy looked up vaguely. "I don't know."

I cursed under my breath. "I'll have to go look for

her. You stay put. On second thought, you'd better come with me so I can watch you."

Reluctantly, Billy left the ants. "She went to see the bears, maybe."

"She can't see the bears. They're in the park, and we aren't there yet."

There were people all over the place, cooking, eating, heading for the pool or back from it, crowding into the store. Ariadne had been wearing a red sunsuit, but half the kids out running around had red somethings on. We passed Harry, and I called, "Come help us look for your little sister."

He waved, but the girl was smiling at him, and he didn't come with us. "Nothing will happen to her with all these people around," he said, and kept on talking to the girl in red shorts.

I snorted. Did he really think all these strangers were going to look out for Ariadne?

We walked from one end of the camp to the other and didn't see her. We met Alison, with an anxious look on her face, when we were almost back to our motorhome.

"I can't find her," I said. "If she's moving, she could be staying just ahead of us."

Alison bit her lip. "And it'll be our fault if anything happens to her. Why didn't you get Harry to help look?"

I rolled my eyes. "Harry's not much use in an emergency. You don't think she could have gone back to the pool house, do you?"

"I hope not. I'll go check there, and you make another pass around the park. This time stop and ask people. Maybe she went in someone else's trailer or something."

Ten minutes later, at the far back of the campground, I stopped. Nobody had seen a little girl in a red sunsuit. I didn't know where else to look, and I was getting pretty nervous.

"Ariadne, where are you?" I yelled in frustration.

To my great surprise, she answered. "I'm here," she said.

I looked all around, but it wasn't until she yelled again that I looked up.

And there was her little face, peering down at me from the top branches of the tallest cedar tree in the camp. About a mile over my head.

My stomach tightened in a knot. She had to be at least thirty feet off the ground.

My mouth went dry. "Come down," I suggested, "and have supper."

"Okay," Ariadne said, and disappeared. A moment later there was a flurry of movement in the branches, and I thought she'd fallen.

"Ariadne?" I asked.

Her voice sounded small. "I can't get down, Lewis. I slid, and my hands hurt."

My teeth came together with an audible click. "How did you get up there?"

"I climbed up to get away from the bears," she said.

"There aren't any bears here," I protested, moving directly under the lower branches. I couldn't even see her when I looked straight up.

"They would bite me," she said, and then I caught a glimpse of red and a few needles drifting down through the branches as she slid down a bit more.

I had visions of her falling all the way and breaking her neck. And guess who'd be held responsible?

I evaluated the tree, swallowed, and called up to her. "Stay where you are, Ariadne. I'll come and get you."

"Can I climb up, too?"

I'd forgotten Billy. "No. You sit down, right there, and wait for me, okay?"

I didn't know if he could be trusted or not, but I *had* to get Ariadne down.

The branches scratched my face and especially my ears as I climbed. It was a long way up, and the branches were getting a little small to hold my weight before I finally got within range of her. She looked scared, and reached out for me.

"If I try to carry you," I told her, "I can't hang on. I need both hands to get down, so I'll stay just a step below you, to catch you if you slip, and you move down one branch at a time. Okay?"

"Okay," Ariadne said. "See, Lewis, there's the bear!"

I looked down, where she was pointing. I might have laughed if I hadn't been so high in the air, still having to get her safely down.

"That's a dog, Ariadne. Not a bear."

"No, I heard that lady call him 'bear,'" she insisted.

"He's just a big dog, and they probably named him Bear because he sort of looks like one. Get ready, now, and put one foot down, okay?"

And then I paused and leaned out a little to see better. Was that a familiar car in that last campsite way up on the side of the hill, almost hidden by a couple of trees?

It was light blue, but I couldn't tell if it was the same car that carried the guy who claimed to have lost his keys near our coach. But now I could tell that this one was towing a small travel trailer.

Ariadne's foot touched my shoulder, and I guided her foot onto a sturdy branch and dropped down one level myself. I hoped we both made it down all right.

It seemed to take forever, and Alison was standing there with Billy when I dropped to the ground, soaked in sweat. I handed Ariadne to her with relief.

"Let's go eat," I said, to cover the fact that my knees were wobbly.

"I think the first sandwiches are probably cold by now," my sister said. "Whatever made her climb up there?"

"A bear," Ariadne insisted, ignoring my explanation. "There! See?"

Even when we paused to talk to the lady who was walking the dog, Ariadne wouldn't believe he was just named Bear, but was a dog, so I gave up.

I glanced over in the direction where I'd seen the

blue car, but I couldn't see it at all from the ground. By this time, though, I realized that we'd seen the same people and the same rigs in each of the campgrounds. A lot of them were heading for Yellowstone, too.

When we got back to the motorhome, Harry was sitting at the picnic table, finishing the last of the sandwiches Alison had made. He hadn't touched the salad.

Alison's lips tightened, though I was glad we were going to get fresh, hot ones. "You might have helped," she said.

Harry grinned. "With all those sandwiches going to waste? Didn't Ma pack some Fig Newtons somewhere? I couldn't find them."

"They were in a box in one of the basement compartments," I said. "That one, I think."

"The keys are in the ignition," Harry said, popping open a Coke and taking a slurp.

Meaning, I took it, that I should fetch the keys and find him the cookies. Alison wasn't the only one gritting her teeth, but I did it.

As I turned the key in the compartment door, I heard a sound that I realized I'd heard earlier, sort of faint and far away. "Sounds like a cat around here somewhere," I commented.

Before I could prop the door open, Billy exploded in my direction. "I want the kitty," he cried.

And sure enough, we had a stowaway.

There he was, the big gray-striped cat Billy had been chasing at the other camp. He leaped past me and right into Billy's arms.

Chapter 6

I looked at Billy accusingly. "Did you know that cat was in the compartment?"

He returned my gaze without speaking, stroking the animal's thick fur with obvious pleasure.

"Did you *put* him in there?" I demanded.

"Billy, that's kidnapping!" Alison said, horrified. "He belongs to the people at the other campground!"

"They weren't taking care of him," Billy said, and though he refused to actually admit anything, we knew he had deliberately taken the cat and put him in the compartment.

We told the Rupes as soon as they came home, after leaving us kids alone all evening. They raved about the steaks the "Nabs," as they called them, had barbecued. I thought about our cheese sandwiches.

Alison told them about the cat.

"The lady at the store said his name was William,"

Billy volunteered. "Same as mine. We need some cat food, Mama. He didn't like the crusts of my sandwich."

"There's tuna in the cupboard. Give him some of that," Mrs. Rupe said. "It's in that top cupboard, Alison."

Alison didn't move. "I'll bet the people who own him are worried about what's happened to him. They probably never saw him again after the fire. They may even think he was killed."

Mrs. Rupe was already reaching for the magazine she'd been reading earlier. "We can leave him off on the way home. We'll be staying at the same campground again." She sat down in the copilot's seat, adjusting the back to a comfortable angle.

"Don't you think we should call them and let them know William's all right?" Alison asked hesitantly.

"He's only a cat," Harry said. "What's the big deal?"

My eyes met Alison's and neither of us said anything more as she got down the tuna and put some on a paper plate. I knew Alison would have given almost anything to have a cat of her own, but if she'd brought home one that belonged to someone else—even if Mom and Dad had allowed her to have one—they would have insisted the owners be notified at once, until it could be returned.

When we got up the next morning, eager to go on to Yellowstone National Park, I couldn't find my glasses.

"Where did you put them?" Alison asked, popping frozen waffles into the toaster for Ariadne.

"The same place I've been keeping them every night since we left home. In my left shoe, under the edge of the couch where nobody could step on them."

Alison's eyes turned toward Billy. He was sitting at the table opposite his little sister, stroking the cat, who seemed perfectly content in his lap.

"Billy, did you take Lewis's glasses?"

His smile was innocent but I knew he was guilty. "Where did you put them? I have to have them, Billy. I can't see without them."

"William wants some more tuna fish," Billy said.

His folks were sitting up front, drinking coffee, and they heard all this. Neither of them turned around or said a word. I felt rage rising up inside of me, and I thought Alison was feeling the same thing, even if they weren't *her* glasses. I reached over and took hold of Billy's ear, pinching it a little.

"What did you do with them, Billy?"

He pretended he didn't hear me, stroking the cat more vigorously until I applied a little more pressure and then began to twist his ear.

When I was in the third grade, we had a teacher named Mrs. Stott. I heard her once telling the sixth-grade teacher that twisting an ear was how she controlled an unruly pupil. "It leaves no marks," she'd said, "but it's usually effective."

It was effective on Billy, too. The angelic smile slid

off his face and he muttered under his breath, "They're in the pocket behind Daddy's seat."

There was a pouch there where the maps were kept. Mr. Rupe kept right on reading the morning paper while I dug out my glasses and inspected them to see if they'd been scratched. I settled them on my nose and felt relieved when everything around me sprang back into sharp focus.

Some fun it would have been riding through Yellowstone without my glasses, I thought, glaring at the back of Billy's head. A moose could have stuck his nose right on the window and I wouldn't have recognized it.

I wasn't disgusted with Billy as much as I was with the rest of the Rupes. They all knew Billy had taken my glasses—my *eyes* practically—and nobody said a word about it.

I didn't think about it very long, though. A lot of the other people from the campground were also going into the park, and the cars, trailers, and motorhomes stretched out in a long line, getting tickets.

The woman in the ranger's uniform handed Mr. Rupe a bunch of maps and papers, and he tossed most of them over his shoulder into Harry's lap. "There, educate yourself," he said.

Harry tossed them to me. "You read this, Lewis," he said. "I just want to get to the good stuff. Where're the bears?"

"I don't like bears," Ariadne said nervously. "They will eat me."

"No, they won't," Alison assured her. "We'll just look at them through the windows, and we'll be perfectly safe."

We crossed the border between Montana and Wyoming—the boundary was inside the park—and I looked down at the top paper of the things the ranger had given us.

It was a bright yellow flyer with big letters across the top. "Warning," it said. "Many visitors have been gored by buffalo. Buffalo can weigh 2,000 pounds and can sprint at 30 miles per hour. These animals may appear tame, but are wild, unpredictable, and dangerous. Do not approach buffalo."

At the bottom of the page was a sketch of a gigantic buffalo tossing a man into the air, with his hat flying one direction and his camera dropping another way.

I read this aloud, and Harry laughed. "Maybe this is going to be interesting after all." I wondered if he was hoping to see someone thrown or trampled, but I was afraid to ask.

"Look at the map," Mr. Rupe said, passing a car in a zone where a sign said NO PASSING. "See which way we should go when we get to an intersection."

I studied the map. "The roads go in two loops," I said after a few moments. "If we turn left and go north, we can see Mammoth Hot Springs and then follow the loop around through the Tower-Roosevelt area and back down to Canyon Village. If we go right at the first intersection, we'll see the paint pots and a lot of the geysers, including Old Faithful. That goes on around what they call West Thumb, around part of Yellowstone Lake and Fishing Bridge, and back up to Canyon Village."

"What's all that stuff?" Harry wanted to know. "Where do we see the animals?"

"It's a park—thirty-four hundred seventy-two square miles of it," I said, reading from one of the brochures. "And the animals run wild all through it. There's no way of knowing where you're going to see animals."

Harry looked astonished. "You mean we came all this way and we might not even see any animals?"

"We just got here," Mr. Rupe said somewhat crossly. "I'm sure there are plenty of animals."

And right after that, Alison lifted Ariadne to stand on the couch as she cried, "Look! There's a whole herd of buffalo!"

There were too many to count, strung out along the river to our left. None of us had ever seen buffalo outside a zoo before, and I immediately thought of the westerns I'd read, when Indians galloped across the plains for their winter food while the big animals thundered ahead of them.

"Look, Billy!" I said, pulling him up beside me. "See the buffalo?"

He glanced out the window, then pulled away. "I want to play with William," he stated.

"They're too far away," Harry complained. "I hope we're going to get closer than this to some of them. I thought we were going to see them right up close."

I was imagining myself riding with the hunters, fitting an arrow to my bow, ready to bring down the meat to feed my family. I didn't want to listen to Harry.

A glance at my sister showed she was thinking that way, too. "Look, Ariadne, there's a baby one," she said, and Ariadne put her nose against the glass to watch as we passed the buffalo and left them behind.

Before we got to Madison, where the road branched, we had seen two does, one buck, and another half-dozen buffalo. None of them was close enough to suit Harry. I was beginning to get tired of Harry.

Billy refused to put down the cat and look out at the wildlife. After a while, I stopped trying to coax him. To heck with the Rupes, I thought. I was going to enjoy this trip in spite of them.

We turned off the main road for the first time at the parking area for the paint pots. It was just about full, and Mr. Rupe decided the only thing to do was to park behind a half-dozen cars, though it was obvious that they couldn't get out until he moved.

"They all came to see this stuff, too," he said, taking the keys out of the ignition. "Let's go take a look."

Harry looked bored. "We have to walk out on that boardwalk? I think I'll stay here and make a sandwich."

"You'll get out and come with the rest of us," Mr. Rupe said. "Move it."

There were warning signs before we got onto the

boardwalk that had been constructed throughout the area:

DANGEROUS THERMAL AREAS: BOILING WATER—THIN CRUSTS. ALWAYS STAY ON CONSTRUCTED WALKWAYS. DRIVE CAREFULLY IN STEAMY AREAS.

IT IS UNLAWFUL TO THROW OBJECTS INTO POOLS, TAKE PETS INTO THERMAL AREAS, FEED OR MOLEST ANIMALS, DEFACE OR REMOVE SPECIMENS FROM THERMAL AREAS, LITTER OR SMOKE IN THERMAL AREAS.

"Uh, Billy, you'd better leave the cat behind," I suggested.

His lower lip jutted out. "I want to take him," he said. "He'll get lonesome by himself."

"Hang on to him tight," Mr. Rupe said. "If he falls into one of these hot pots, it'll cook him."

Alison and I seemed to be exchanging glances pretty often. The Rupes didn't appear to think the signs and warnings referred to *them,* and after what Mr. Rupe had said, I didn't see how I could insist on leaving William behind.

Because Billy needed both arms to hold the cat, it wasn't even possible to hold his hand while we walked, the way Alison was doing with Ariadne. And we hadn't gone very far along the wooden walkway before it began to make me very nervous.

The land around us looked like alkali desert in the old Zane Grey novels my grandpa stored in his attic, except that in a lot of places steam was coming out of the ground. And then we were in the middle of the paint pots.

Even Harry was a little bit impressed by them. "Hey, weird!" he commented. "Pink mud!"

It was not only pale pink, it was boiling hot. The mud was thick and made bubbles that sort of burped and sent globs up in the air and even onto the edge of the walkway. I couldn't hold on to Billy's hand, but I felt safer resting a hand on his shoulder. At least he didn't resist that.

The paint pots were mostly sunk into pits in the ground, but the contents bubbled hard enough to bring them splattering out of the tops of the holes. There was pale orange, and a sort of yellowish tan, and a grayish blue. I wondered what the first explorers who saw them had thought. All over the whole area there was steam in the air, drifting and blowing enough to carry its warmth to us.

Alison grinned at me. "Neat, aren't they?" she said.

We went on around the paint pots, and circled back to rejoin the main walkway to the parking lot. Right after we'd passed a sign that cautioned STAY ON THE WALKS Harry suddenly stepped off into a little trickle of a stream and dipped his hand into the water.

"It's warm enough to take a bath in," he marveled.

An older couple stared at him disapprovingly, but it didn't bother Harry. "No problem getting off there," he said, loud enough for the couple to hear him. "There's no boiling water."

I muttered under my breath to Alison. "Let's pretend we don't know him."

"For sure," she murmured back. And then, looking ahead, she frowned a little. "Lewis, isn't that the car that's been right behind us practically all the way here?"

"The blue Crown Victoria?" I said before I got so much as a glance at it.

"Yes. Do you . . . think it's kind of suspicious?"

Harry overheard that and turned to speak to us. "What's to be suspicious about? Half the cars from Missoula on were coming to Yellowstone, weren't they?"

"They stayed in an RV park with no RV," I said slowly. "And then they got a trailer and kept on behind us. I *think* it's the same car. I remember the license number. Let's check it out."

"It's the same car where that guy was who said he lost his keys near our motorhome. The ones Lewis found in *our* coach," Alison said, and now it was out in the open, not just in my own mind.

"Like Ma said, Billy probably found them and took them inside," Harry pointed out.

Billy, with William draped over his shoulder, scowled and said, "I didn't."

"Ariadne, then," Harry said.

"What?" Ariadne demanded.

"Found the guy's lost keys and took them into the motorhome."

"No," Ariadne said. "I didn't have any keys."

Harry swept a careless glance over their faces. "You're compulsive liars, both of you," he said, and jogged on ahead, leaving us to deal with the insulted denials.

Mr. and Mrs. Rupe got back to the coach before we did, and before we reached them we realized that several angry tourists were swarming around like bees ready to sting. They didn't like the way the motorhome was parked so they couldn't move their cars.

"It was pretty darned inconsiderate, pinning us in like this," one man was saying as we walked up.

"We were only gone about twenty-five minutes," Mr. Rupe defended himself.

"Yeah, and we've been held up for twenty minutes waiting to get out. Get that thing out of the way, will you?"

It was embarrassing. I wondered if Mr. Rupe was as inconsiderate of his customers at the bank as he'd been of people on this trip. "Watch Billy again," I told Alison. "I'm going to walk over and check out that license plate."

Harry didn't seem to be embarrassed. In fact, he said rudely to one of the protesters, "Hold your horses, mister, we have to load up everybody first."

I trotted past the people who were listening to the exchange over the parking, took a quick look, and returned to whisper as we climbed into the coach. "Same license number," I said. "And that one guy sure looks familiar, but I can't think where I saw him first. Besides in the car, I mean, coming out of the Columbia River Gorge."

"Really?" Alison moved over to peer out the window to where two men were getting into the Crown Victoria. "Hmm. He looks familiar to me, too. I think . . . maybe we saw him in a uniform, or a uniform cap or something . . ."

That was enough to trigger my memory. "He's the guy—" I began, but at that moment Mr. Rupe climbed in, slammed the door, and practically knocked us down getting into the driver's seat.

"Sit down," he barked at us kids, and then said to his wife, "What a bunch of soreheads. Where else was I supposed to park? There was no more room."

I forgot about the Rupes for the moment.

I knew where I'd seen the man who had dropped the keys. I couldn't wait to talk to my sister about it, and I wondered how long it would take to get her alone to do it.

Chapter 7

Getting a few minutes alone with my sister was hard to do. None of the Rupes ever took charge of Billy and Ariadne at all. If Alison even took time to go to the bathroom, they were unsupervised and got into trouble, unless *I* held on to them.

From the time we left home, we'd both caught Billy digging into other people's luggage and purses and private belongings. He just seemed to be curious, and he didn't actually hurt anything, but we didn't feel as if we could let him do it. I stopped him from stuffing the cat into the map pocket on the back of the driver's seat. I rescued the Cheerios when Ariadne tried to dump them all out for the birds. I even picked up one of Mrs. Rupe's cigarettes after it fell out of an ash tray onto the table, where it left a brown burn mark.

Those things all happened before we left the paint

pot parking area. We waited for a private moment after we turned off on a side road.

"When we get out," Alison said softly, "let's hang behind everybody else, okay?"

We tried. There were shallow lakes, filled with colorful algae and with steam rising from them, and signs saying not to throw anything into the water.

"How hot is that water?" Harry asked. "I'm going to see how fast some ice cubes will melt," and he got out a plastic bag to hold them.

"Hey, this is neat!" he said a moment later when the ice disappeared the moment it hit the surface of the nearest lake. "You want to dump some in, Billy?"

This time Billy'd left the cat in the coach, so he dumped in ice cubes and went back for more. Alison, holding tightly to Ariadne so she couldn't possibly fall into the hot water, rolled her eyes at me.

Then she straightened up and looked past me with a sober expression. "They're still with us. The guys in the blue car."

"I remembered where I saw that guy before, the passenger, the one who *lost* his keys in our coach," I said.

"So did I," Alison said. "In a uniform shirt and cap. He's the one who tried to trade a different motor home for the one we already had. The name on his shirt was Syd."

I nodded. "Right. Funny, how someone in uniform looks different in other clothes. I don't know why it took so long for me to realize why he looked familiar. So why's the guy from the RV rental place following us?"

"He *might* not be following us," Alison said cautiously. "He might just have been coming here in the first place."

"And Harry might follow all the rules," I said. "Not likely. I've been thinking about it ever since we left the paint pots. Syd whatever-his-name-is wanted to exchange motorhomes, and probably anybody but the Rupes would have done it. So why is it important enough for them to follow us and try to get inside *this* one?"

"The money Billy found," Alison said, stealing my idea. "If he picked up that hundred-dollar bill in the motorhome, maybe there's more hidden there."

"A new employee didn't read the papers carefully enough and just took one that was the right model. When the guys who hid the money in this one discovered what had happened, they tried to trade back, and when Mr. Rupe refused, they came after us. You know, I heard that man snooping around that first morning, and he came back several times hoping to sneak in. He probably knows right where the money is hidden."

"Do you think he had something to do with the fire that night at the campground?" Alison asked. "Like maybe he set it to create a diversion so we'd all leave the motorhome unlocked while we went to look at the fire?"

I hadn't thought of that angle yet, but I nodded as

if I had. "And when I went chasing after Billy, the guy was over there by our rig. He was probably the only person in the whole camp who wasn't curious about the fire."

"So what are we going to do? Do you think there's any point in telling Mr. and Mrs. Rupe?"

We looked at each other and rejected that idea without further discussion. "What should we do, then?"

"Try to find the money. Billy could probably tell us where it is, if he would. He must have poked into every cranny in the whole rig." I glanced over to where Harry was lifting Billy onto a railing, where he balanced him right above the steaming water. "Jeez, if he lets Billy fall—"

"Let's see if we can get Billy to walk with us," Alison suggested, "before he gets boiled alive."

It wasn't a joke. We got really nervous, watching, and it was a relief when Harry swung his little brother down onto the boardwalk again.

The men in the blue car had parked on the edge of the road, but they didn't get out and look at anything. I wished I was driving so I could take some maneuvers to prove, once and for all, that they *were* following us. If it had been Dad, I'd have bet he'd have felt the same, but Mr. Rupe probably wouldn't even listen to me.

So we finally went on around the loop—everything at Yellowstone seemed to be on a loop, so you didn't have to turn around and go back the way you'd come—and headed on to see Old Faithful.

All around in the distance there were geysers and steam vents. I knew it would be dangerous—and forbidden—to walk out and look at them up close, but I imagined what it would be like. I wished Mom and Dad had brought us here, instead of the Rupes; I knew with them we would have found out a lot more about the whole park. The Rupes didn't seem to want to know anything.

When we turned in at the road to Old Faithful Lodge, I caught a glimpse of a light blue car just ready to turn behind us. Of course Old Faithful was the most famous landmark in the whole park, so probably everybody stopped here, but my heart was thudding as we cruised into the lot, looking for a place to park.

It was a huge area, and there were people walking in every direction. Mr. Rupe almost ran into a couple of teenagers who darted out from behind a bus. He swore and slammed on the brakes. They gave him the finger, and Mrs. Rupe said, "Kids have no manners these days."

The lot was crowded enough that there wasn't much maneuvering room, and Mr. Rupe had a terrible time trying to get the big coach into a parking spot. He clipped somebody's mirror and pushed it out of place, and almost backed into a car that was trying to pull out. Finally he gave up and drove to the very back of the lot. There, there were several spaces next to each other, and he managed to park right in the middle of them, taking up four car spaces.

"This way," he said with satisfaction, "nobody's likely to run into us."

My eyes were getting tired from rolling them back in my head.

Mrs. Rupc had scanned the signs around us while all this was going on. "There's a general store and a photo shop—you can get some film, Milton, and get pictures of Old Faithful—and I think there's a place to buy lunch, too."

Alison and I were the last ones off the coach. She gave me a worried look. "Do you think those guys will try to break in while we're gone? They may even have a duplicate key from the RV place."

"I don't know. I don't see how we can stop them. So far I think they've only tried to get in when the motorhome was unlocked. If I didn't want to see Old Faithful myself, I'd stay here and guard it."

"I'd be very nervous about you staying here alone," Alison said. "I think those people have to be crooks. I'll bet they stole the money they hid in here. Maybe you can get Billy to tell you where it is, Lewis."

But Billy denied that he knew where there was any more money. He said he didn't remember where the hundred-dollar bill had come from. Harry overheard the end of our conversation and offered to carry the money Billy already had, but Billy shook his head. "It's mine," he said.

There didn't seem to be anything to do except get out and go with the others. I looked around for the blue car and saw it several rows ahead. Nobody had gotten out of it yet.

It was harder to keep it in view when I was down on the ground. As we crossed through that row, though, I could tell there were still two people in it. And when I looked back a minute later, they were gone.

"I'm going to duck back for a minute," I hissed to Alison. "If I don't catch up before you get there, I'll meet you at the general store, okay?"

She looked worried. "Don't take any chances, Lewis. You aren't the hero type."

That stung. I stared after her for a few seconds as they all moved on, wondering why she'd had to say that. I knew I wasn't an athletic champion, but that didn't mean I couldn't do something heroic.

I wasn't an idiot, however. I wasn't about to have a confrontation with two grown men. I saw them already. As I'd suspected, they'd gone in the direction of our motorhome, which pretty well proved to me that our suspicions were on target. Everybody else was walking toward either the cluster of buildings where we were headed or on down the path toward the famous geyser.

Right while I watched, mostly hidden behind a brown van, one of the men shook the door handle. It was locked, of course. Even Mr. Rupe wasn't stupid enough to leave it open. And it didn't look as if the men had an extra key for it.

I hoped they wouldn't dare force the lock, not there in broad daylight with people all around.

Alison and the Rupes had disappeared, and not knowing what else to do, I ran in the direction they'd gone.

The Rupes hadn't missed me, and Alison looked relieved when I showed up right near the stove.

"They tried the door, but I think they gave up," I said to her under my breath when I got close. "Boy, this place has a lot of stuff, huh?" I added as we stepped in the door.

We bought some souvenirs to take home—a Yellowstone cup for Dad, a bracelet for Mom, and I got a black T-shirt with a neat wolf's head on the front of it, and YELLOWSTONE printed underneath. Alison got one in dark blue with a bison on it.

I also bought a guidebook for the park. Harry, who had money enough to pick out anything he wanted, got two T-shirts, a sweatshirt, three rolls of film, and a giant chocolate bar. He grimaced at me. "You really got a thing about books, don't you? Even on vacation."

"I figure I came all this way, I might as well know what I'm seeing," I said, wishing he'd shut up. I'd considered and rejected the idea of sharing our suspicions with Harry. He'd probably laugh at us.

We lined up to pick out our lunches, and I chose a double cheeseburger, fries, and a big Coke. So did Billy.

"You'll never eat that much," his mother told him. "Get a children's burger and a small order of fries."

His lower lip came out. "I want the same thing Lewis and Harry are having."

"I'm having a double burger," Harry said cheerfully.

"I want the same thing as Lewis, then," Billy insisted, and they let him get it.

He couldn't carry his tray to the table, though, so Harry carried it for him. Just before he got there, he stopped to keep from running into Alison, who was carrying Ariadne's tray. The giant Coke tilted and slid off, dumping it and the two cups of ice cubes in it into Mr. Rupe's lap.

He sprang up with an oath and nearly overturned the little table.

The people beyond him scrambled to get out of his way, and he didn't bother to apologize. His face was red and he looked as if he'd wet his pants. I was glad I hadn't been the one to have the accident when he read the riot act to Harry so everybody in the place was looking at us.

When things sort of settled down again, I ate my lunch, flipping through my guidebook to see what it said about Old Faithful. Anything to change the subject.

"It says the Washburn Party discovered it in 1870. It erupts more often than any other geyser. The eruptions last from two to five minutes, and it's the most famous feature of the park."

None of the Rupes reacted to this information. Finally Alison said, "I hope it goes off right after we get there."

"Yeah," Harry echoed. "Let's get going."

Mrs. Rupe gathered up her packages. "Why don't you boys take this stuff back to the motorhome so we don't have to carry it around."

"Hey, no, Ma," Harry protested. "What if the geyser goes off while we're doing that?"

"I'll go," I said quickly. I didn't know what I could do if I caught the guys from the blue car breaking into the motorhome, but I wanted to know what they were up to.

So I hurried back to the coach with all the things we'd bought, but the men weren't there. On the way back, after unloading all the bags, I saw why.

Somebody in a mini motorhome, no better at driving an RV than Mr. Rupe, had attempted to back out of a parking space and crunched in the front fender of the blue Crown Victoria. Two elderly ladies and the two men were standing there in the hot sun, and they all seemed rather agitated.

I grinned a little, glad the men were going to be busy (maybe, I hoped, while some park ranger checked out the situation?) while we were gone.

I got to the others just in time to see Old Faithful beginning to erupt. It came up in a little squirt, and everybody began to get their cameras into position, including Harry, and then it died away for a minute or so while everybody in the crowd held their breaths. It did that several times, and each time Harry snapped pictures before there was anything to see that was more than a few feet high. And then it shot high up into the air, higher and higher, while the tourists oohed and aahed and shutters were clicking all around us.

"Oh, shoot, I ran out of film!" Harry said, about a minute later. "I have to reload! I'll miss the rest of it!"

I didn't have a camera—Dad refused to let us take his good Nikon—so I'd already bought postcards.

It was a good eruption, high in the air, and it lasted long enough for everyone to get a good look and pictures. I was impressed to think this happened, the water spouting out of the ground, twenty times or more every day. But Harry slung the camera back around his neck and said, "Is that all there is to it?"

"So much for the wonders of nature," I muttered to Alison as the crowd began to disperse.

She dismissed Harry with a glance. "Lewis," she said quietly, "what are we going to do about the guys who are following us? Should we call Dad, do you think, and ask his advice?"

"And have him take time off from work and come get us before we see the rest of the park?" I asked. "He can't do anything for us from home, and he probably would have to give up his own vacation time to come. Mr. Rupe's a terrible driver, but so far he hasn't done any serious damage to anything. He'll probably get us home okay eventually."

Her expression didn't change; it was still worried. "But what if they're dangerous?"

"There's only so much they can do when there are always so many people around. I think," I said slowly, "maybe we ought to look for the money, if that's what it is, that's hidden in the coach. Then if it turns up, we can find a cop and report it, and let the authorities decide who it belongs to."

About that time Billy decided he wanted an ice cream cone, and we all headed back to the stand where we could get some. Mr. Rupe paid for them all, so we didn't have to use any of our own money.

When we got back to the motorhome Ariadne had chocolate ice cream dripping off both elbows because she'd bitten the bottom out of her cone, so Alison hurried her off to clean her up. I hesitated long enough to look for the blue Crown Victoria.

It was gone. But I didn't think we'd seen the last of it.

Chapter 8

If it hadn't been for the Rupes, Yellowstone would have been a blast.

Of course, without the Rupes, we'd never have been there, so we made the best of it.

Harry was bored with geysers and paint pots after the first ones. Billy preferred to play with William, Ariadne listened when we showed her things and explained them, and Mr. and Mrs. Rupe annoyed the other tourists by their lack of consideration and by Mrs. Rupe's cigarette butts, which she dropped throughout the park.

Harry kept demanding that we see a bear. I think partly he was teasing his little sister because she was afraid of bears, but mostly he was used to getting what he wanted without waiting for it.

Unfortunately the bears didn't cooperate. We saw elk, though—magnificent animals that grazed within a few yards of us, unperturbed. It was as if they knew they were safe within the park: they ignored us until Mrs. Rupe approached too close to snap a picture; then the bull moved off and the cows followed.

We saw literally hundreds of buffalo. Several times we got held up because one of the great shaggy beasts was ambling up the middle of a narrow road and we couldn't get past it.

I could see people in other vehicles snapping pictures and peering out in interest. Ariadne pressed close to Alison. "Will it bite me?" she asked.

There were a few mule deer, too. It was different seeing them in the wild than it had been watching them in a zoo. It was kind of exciting to have a wild animal come right up alongside of the coach.

"Wait until I stop," Mr. Rupe said to Harry. "These windows, except for the windshield, are all tinted. You won't get good pictures through the darker glass."

Harry didn't pay any attention. When an animal came in sight, he began clicking away. Billy looked if they were really close, but mostly he was still more interested in the cat. I wondered if his folks were going to return it to the campground owners, or if they'd let him take it home with them.

Mrs. Rupe said it was too tiring to drive around the park all day, every day. So by about midafternoon, the first day and every day after, we headed back for the camp. There the little kids could swim or use the playground equipment (with Alison watching them every minute, of course) and Harry could play video games and swim. Mr. and Mrs. Rupe went over to the Nabs to play cards or watch a movie on the VCR that they didn't think was suitable for Billy and Ariadne.

"I'm surprised they care," Alison commented to me. "They don't seem to care about much else the kids do."

"More likely," I suggested, "they go over there just to get away from the kids. It's too noisy when they're here."

Alison gave me a wry grin. "Are you getting cynical, Lewis?"

I thought about it and nodded. "Yeah. I guess I am."

As much of the time as we could, Alison and I poked around in the motorhome trying to find a spot that might conceal a quantity of hundred-dollar bills.

There were lots of nooks and crannies, actually. There were strange little empty spaces in the corners of cupboards and behind the couch and in the map pouches. There were lots of drawers and doors everywhere that opened onto big compartments and small ones, and some that opened on fuse boxes and had no hiding places at all. There was space in the closet, and behind the little TV that pulled out on a shelf in the bedroom, and beneath the clothes basket behind one of the doors, and there was a flap of carpet in the bedroom that folded back to reveal a safe set into the floor. It was just a hiding place, really, like a can set into the floor. I got excited when I found that, but when I got it open, it was disappointingly empty.

Billy walked in before I got it closed. "What's that?" he asked.

"A hiding place. I'm trying to find some more of that money you found, Billy. Maybe you can help me."

An expression crossed his face that I couldn't describe, but it sent a prickle up my back. "You probably don't remember where you got it, though, right?"

"Right," Billy said. Another disappointment. But somehow I was convinced he *did* know where the hundred-dollar bill had come from.

"Were there a whole lot of bills, where you found the other one?"

It was no use. Billy shrugged. "I don't know," he said.

If money had been hidden in one of the compartments under the coach, I was out of luck. They could be opened only from outside the motorhome, and I didn't have the keys. And from what I remembered when we were loading, I thought they were just big open areas where there weren't any hiding places. Besides, I didn't see how Billy would have had access to them. The money had to have been hidden inside the coach.

It wouldn't necessarily have to be a large place. If the money was all in hundreds, quite a few would fit into a small space. But we couldn't find it.

We kept seeing the blue car. It was even easier to spot now because it had a crumpled fender. The men in it never seemed to be paying any attention to us, but every time we looked around, there they were. Once we were close enough to hear them talking, and we learned the second man's name was Ernie. He had a bushy mustache, and he had even less interest in geysers and colored lakes than the Rupes did.

They were there our second day in the park when we watched a geyser spouting up from the middle of a lake, and when Mrs. Rupe was taking pictures of Gibbon Falls, again at the Grand Geyser where the hot water spouted without warning into a crystal fan several hundred feet high, and at the Sapphire Pool where the water was a gorgeous shade of deep blue.

The men were always there, but they weren't looking at the scenery. They were hovering around the motorhome, and I kept wondering how brave they'd be about getting into it if it was left unlocked and unattended for a few minutes.

Mr. Rupe usually locked it up, though, unless we were standing right within sight of it. It must have been pretty frustrating for Syd and Ernie because they probably wouldn't have needed long to get what they wanted and get away with it.

"If these guys know where the money is hidden," I said thoughtfully to Alison in one of the few times we got to talk privately, "I wonder why they didn't get it when the one dropped his keys. And why did he

THE ABSOLUTELY TRUE STORY . . .

drop the keys? He must have heard them land, even on the carpet."

"Maybe he got surprised and was afraid of being caught, so he didn't take time to pick them up but just ran. Lewis, we really ought to talk to an adult about this. It could be quite serious."

We even discussed whether we had learned enough to try to explain it to Mr. Rupe. We hadn't decided yet when he did the most stupid thing of all, which made the decision for us.

Harry was the one who yelped in excitement when we came upon about a dozen buffalo grazing right at the edge of the road, above a small stream. "Hey, stop, Dad! I should be able to get some good pictures of these!"

He jumped out of the motorhome almost before it had stopped, and we watched through the window as he raised the camera to look into it, only about twenty feet from a big old bull. It was easy to believe that he weighed a ton.

The yellow warning sheet was lying right on the end of the couch where Harry had been sitting, but he had forgotten all about it. "Hey, Dad, aren't you going to get some pictures, too?"

"I'm coming," Mr. Rupe said, and armed with his own camera he followed after Harry.

"Be careful, Milton," Mrs. Rupe called out the open window. "Don't get too close."

"Ah, these babies are used to having their pictures

taken," her husband assured her. "They're tame, all the animals in this place are, because they know they're safe. Billy, stay in the coach."

My mouth had gone dry. According to the yellow warning sheet, the animals weren't tame at all. They just weren't afraid of people or cars, so they didn't run away, but they'd been known to attack tourists who bothered them.

So far Mr. Rupe and Harry didn't seem to be bothering these buffalo; they kept on grazing. Harry ran out of film about then. He always took a lot of pictures before he got into a position to get the best ones, and then had to reload about the time he could have taken the best shot.

He had just jumped back into the motorhome when Mrs. Rupe said sharply through the open window, "Milton, be careful!"

The big bull had suddenly raised its massive head and was staring right at Mr. Rupe, who had walked up to about ten feet from the bull. He was closer to the bull than to the open door of the coach.

He didn't take the camera away from his eye. "Oh, this ought to make a terrific shot," he said, and clicked away.

I could see the bull's eyes, kind of reddish looking, and mean. I definitely thought he looked mean.

I heard Alison's near-whisper right alongside me. "He's crazy. That thing could kill him."

Just then a car pulled in right ahead of us, and a uniformed ranger got out. The small herd of buffalo, including the big bull, began to move off down the slope toward the stream.

"Sir, I'll have to ask you to get back into your vehicle," the ranger said. "It isn't safe to get that close to an animal."

Mrs. Rupe closed the window, so we couldn't hear what they said after that. But I watched as a red stain crept up Mr. Rupe's face while the ranger lectured him. Mr. Rupe was angry and embarrassed when he finally got back into the driver's seat and we moved on.

Nobody said anything, but instead of going on, we went back to the campground. The Nabakowskis had returned to camp early, too, and the adults gathered around their picnic table and got out some game. As far as I could tell, the Rupes never even glanced over toward their kids. No wonder they'd wanted Alison to come along and take care of them.

We ate a late lunch and then we all swam for a while. On the way back, Harry stopped and fell into conversation with the girl in the red shorts, whose name was Peggy. Alison and I settled the kids in at the table to color. Alison had brought a shoe box with art supplies, scissors, and crayons. She went to put the top back on the box, then frowned.

"What happened to my Scotch tape? Have you kids been in my box?"

"Gone, gone, gone," Ariadne said in a singsong voice.

"Gone where? Ariadne, did you take my Scotch tape?"

Ariadne smiled sweetly. "Gone," she repeated.

"What did you do with it?" Alison demanded.

The little girl shook her head. "I don't know."

Alison's eyes met mine. "That phrase seems to get them off the hook for practically anything. I need the tape, kids. If you know where it is, please give it back."

Billy had the cat draped over his shoulder again. It must have been used to little kids or it wouldn't have tolerated the things he did with it. "I need the red," he said, and took that crayon away from his sister.

Alison left them at the table and started picking up odds and ends that had been left lying around. There was a book on Mrs. Rupe's copilot's seat, and when she picked it up to set it on the console, she made a sound of disgust.

"What's the matter?" I asked. I gathered all the park information, debated leaving the yellow sheet warning about the dangerous buffalo on top, then decided I'd better hide it in the middle. I didn't want Mr. Rupe to stay in a bad mood forever.

She held up the book so I could see it. Mrs. Rupe had marked her place with a lighted cigarette. It had gone out, but not before it had scorched the edges of quite a few pages.

"Mom and Dad would have a fit if they knew what the Rupes are really like," she murmured. "I know Mom felt she knew them, but she didn't, really. She only saw them at church and for a few minutes when they came over to borrow something."

"Yeah," I agreed. "And Dad only saw Mr. Rupe at

the bank and the bowling alley. He never saw him drive. I just hope we get home in one piece." I glanced over to where Billy had lowered William onto his lap, where the cat seemed to have dozed off in comfort even though it hung off his legs on both sides. I kept my voice low. "Alison, we're going to have to tell somebody about that car that's following us, and that we think there may be a lot of money hidden in this thing. For all we know, we might be in the middle of a situation that's as dangerous as the one Mr. Rupe was in with that buffalo."

"Maybe we could talk to a ranger," Alison said, almost whispering. "They're the closest thing there is to cops here in the park."

"Not too bad an idea," I agreed, "except how do we catch one of them? There haven't been many around, except in cars that don't stop unless you're doing something stupid or you jump in the middle of the road and flag them down. I can imagine trying to talk to that one this morning with Mr. Rupe listening. He'd want to know why we hadn't told him first, and I still think he probably wouldn't take us seriously."

"And if he acted like we were nuts, the ranger would think so, too."

"But what if somebody gets hurt if we don't tell?"

Alison bit her lip. "It could happen, couldn't it? If Syd and Ernie are desperate enough, they could be nasty." She sighed. "Maybe we should just get away from the motorhome, make sure it's unlocked, and let them get what they want, and forget it. Except if there's something illegal going on, Dad would say we have a responsibility to see that they don't get away with it."

"He might," I began, and then forgot what I was going to say when William the cat exploded, yowling and snarling as he spilled off Billy's lap.

It sounded like he was being killed, and for a few seconds I was too chicken to dive after him when he spurted between us and tried frantically to hide under one of the seats.

Then it registered what I'd seen, and I turned and glared at Billy. He was staring after William, half-excited, half-scared, and I knew what had happened to Alison's Scotch tape.

Chapter 9

"I can't believe this cat slept through being wrapped in almost a whole roll of Scotch tape," Alison declared, snipping again with the scissors. "And I'm ashamed of you, Billy. That was a cruel thing to do to William. When he woke up all tied up, it scared him half to death."

"Not to mention what it did to the rest of us," I added. We'd decided we couldn't pull the tape off; it was hard enough just to hold the cat and trim his hair off under each section of tape we cut loose. "I've got scratches all over my hands from trying to pull him out from under your mom's seat."

"It didn't hurt him," Billy protested. "I tried some on myself, and it didn't hurt."

"It would hurt if we pulled it loose. It's caught in all his hair. And it wasn't your Scotch tape to play with. It was *mine*."

"Buy some more," Billy suggested. He obviously wasn't understanding any of our objections.

"I don't have the money to buy any more," Alison told him, and snipped again. William struggled and nearly got away from me, and I got another scratch across my arm. "I spent all my money on souvenirs, so I can't buy anything now."

Watching Billy think made me feel like I could actually see the little wheels going around in his head.

"I've got some money," he said. And he reached into his pants pocket and handed her a hundred-dollar bill.

Alison forgot to keep cutting Scotch tape out of the cat's fur and I almost let go of him.

"Billy," I said carefully, "didn't you spend some of that hundred dollars on ice cream?"

"I don't know," Billy said.

"He did," Alison remembered. "This has to be a different hundred-dollar bill. Billy, where are you getting this money?"

"I found it," Billy said.

"Where?" Alison demanded, and I asked, "Here? Since we've been at Yellowstone?"

"Lewis, we've got to tell Mr. Rupe."

"No! Daddy can't have it! It's mine! Harry said finders keepers, and I found it!"

"That's okay if it was a quarter, or maybe even a dollar bill," I said, getting a firmer grip on the cat. "But this is too much money. Show us where you found it, Billy."

Well, we tried. We couldn't believe he really didn't remember where he found it, but he wouldn't admit to anything. He was into everything, all the time, when the rest of us weren't paying much attention. He poked into purses and cupboards and compartments until someone—usually Alison—made him stop. The money could have been hidden anywhere inside the coach that he could reach or climb up to.

About the time we got the last of the tape off William, and he'd retired under the chair to lick at his damaged fur, Harry showed up, and we told him what had happened.

He thought the bit with the Scotch tape was funny, and that the hundred-dollar bills were exciting.

"Bring us some more, Billy," he urged, ripping open a new bag of corn chips. He dug into them without offering them around, but I didn't even care.

"No," Billy said flatly.

"Your folks will have to be told about this," I said.

Harry chewed and swallowed. "What do you think Dad's going to do about it? He'll make him tell where they came from, maybe. Is there a lot more, Billy?"

"You don't think your folks will let him keep it, do you?" Alison asked.

"Harry," I said, "I think it's time we told you what's going on." So I did.

Harry forgot to eat for a few minutes. "No kidding. If they had money hid in here, no wonder they wanted to trade coaches. Except why did they let us have this one in the first place?"

"Maybe they told the truth about that much. A new employee made a mistake and brought us the wrong coach."

"I wonder why they'd have hidden money in a rental motor home? They must have planned to take it somewhere. Out of state, maybe, or even over the border into Canada. Or maybe across the Mexican border."

"It just about has to be something illegal, don't you think?" Alison asked.

Harry grinned. "Cripes. Just like in a movie. And you think these guys have been following us, huh? Trying to get in here and get their money back?"

"If it was legitimate," I mused, "all they'd have to do is tell us they'd made a mistake and come and get the money. We all know it doesn't belong to *us*."

Harry got a can of pop out of the refrigerator and popped the top. "I wonder if they'd give us a reward?"

"I don't believe you," Alison said after she'd given a ladylike snort. Ariadne spilled her crayons on the floor, and my sister went to help pick them up, turning her back on Harry.

I stared at him. "What do you think we should do?"

He took a long swallow of root beer. "The next time they show up alongside of us, walk over and ask them what the heck they want and if they know where it's hidden. They'll just about have to give us a reward if we help them, won't they?"

Alison dropped the last crayon into the box. "It doesn't matter to you that it's probably stolen money?"

"Why do you think it has to be illegal?" Harry pressed, flopping down on the couch.

"Because of the way Syd and Ernie are acting. Anybody carrying a lot of money—legitimately—would use better sense than to pack it into a crack somewhere in a rental motorhome. They'd have it in travelers checks or a certified check, not cash."

Harry's brain workings were almost as transparent as Billy's. "Okay," he said, nodding. "Let's go talk to them the next time we see them."

"That might be dangerous," I said mildly, but the idea was kind of exciting, too. I felt a little cowardly that I hadn't done it on my own.

"In the middle of the crowds that are always around? Nah," Harry said confidently.

"And if they say there's money that belongs to them, and we let them come and get it, we just let them walk away with it even if it's stolen?" Alison asked.

Harry showed his teeth in a wicked grin. "After they pay us the reward, of course."

"You know, Harry"—I said what I was thinking before *thinking*, if you know what I mean—"your sense of ethics is lousy. My dad believes that if you let somebody get away with something that's wrong, that makes you guilty, too."

It wouldn't have surprised me if he'd been really irritated with that statement. He wasn't, though. And why *that* should have been a surprise, after what we'd seen of the whole Rupe family, I don't know.

Harry laughed. "*I* didn't steal anything. And hey, if the guy says it's his money, what do I know?"

"Don't you think we should tell your dad what we know and what we suspect then?" Alison asked.

"I only got to be twelve years old," Harry said, "by telling my dad as little as possible. He doesn't have much sense of humor, so if you guess wrong about what you tell him, you suffer for it. What he doesn't know doesn't hurt you, right?"

We gave up. But I kept thinking about walking right up to the guys who were following us and asking them why, and it made my heart beat faster and my mouth get dry.

Harry sure wasn't going to worry about it. He was a real clown the rest of the day. He could be very funny, and we all laughed a lot. Mr. and Mrs. Rupe and the Nabs were going into town to dinner, so we were allowed to buy chicken and broasted potatoes and cole slaw from the store for our supper.

While Alison was giving Ariadne a bath she asked us to watch Billy, and I suggested to Harry that we walk over to the back of the campground, past the blue car and its little trailer.

"What's the matter, scared to go look by yourself?" he taunted, but he came along. I told myself I wasn't being scared of anything, I just thought he might like to come, but I wasn't sure if that was true or not.

When we passed the final stand of trees, the Crown Victoria was there, unhooked from the little trailer. There was no sign of the two men who'd been traveling in it. We stopped and stared. From this point, no other rig was in sight; we were hidden in the little grove of trees.

"They must've gone up to the store or the showers," Harry said. "Let's check it out."

"It's a rental trailer," I pointed out, looking at the license plate and the holder for it. "They rented it in Montana, not back in Washington. If they knew they were coming all the way up here, why didn't they bring a trailer from home? You'd think they would have. They work for an RV rental place."

"They didn't know it would take them this long to get their money back," Harry said readily, approaching close to the trailer and peeking in a window. "And they didn't like sleeping in their car that first night. When we didn't all get diverted away from the motorhome by the fire they set, if they did that, they rented the trailer at the place where they needed it. Boy, I'm glad we're not traveling in this thing! Crummy, isn't it?"

"I want to see, too," Billy insisted, so I held him up to look through the window.

It wasn't exactly crummy, just small and ordinary. No queen-size bed, just a couple of narrow bunks. And no microwave, no full-size refrigerator/freezer, no ice maker. Hardly enough room for two people to get into it at the same time.

"They didn't get this one for comfort," I said,

drawing back from the window and setting Billy on the ground. "It's only a place to sleep until they get what they want."

"So tomorrow," Harry said cheerfully, "let's put an end to it. Come on, Billy, get out of their car. They might catch us poking into their stuff and be mad about it." He slammed the car door after he'd dragged his little brother out of the front seat. "Yep, we can probably clear this all up tomorrow just by talking to them."

It sounded good. I hoped it worked out, even if Harry didn't agree with Alison and me about letting them take the money if they knew where it was hidden. I wondered if Dad would make us go to the police later, after we told him the story. I wished none of it was happening, except seeing Yellowstone.

The next morning started off with Mr. Rupe in a tight-lipped rage because he couldn't find his glasses.

"I put them right there on the console," he said furiously. "I told you to put them in an overhead compartment," Mrs. Rupe said, lighting her first cigarette of the day.

"Who took my glasses?" Mr. Rupe's angry gaze swept across all of us, and even though I wasn't guilty I shrank away from him. He wasn't a good-looking man to begin with, and when his face turned red he was positively homely. Even his bald head was red.

I knew who had most likely taken the glasses. I looked at Billy, but he was absorbed in William. The cat had forgiven him for the Scotch tape episode, or maybe he didn't realize Billy had done it while he was sleeping.

Billy stroked the cat over the fur that had uneven chunks where Alison had cut it to get the tape loose. Billy crooned softly, and William purred loud enough to hear from six feet away.

"Listen up, gang," Mr. Rupe said. "You better all get looking for those glasses, because we're not going anywhere until I have them."

With that he stomped outside and began to unhook the electrical connections.

Mrs. Rupe sighed in exasperation. "I *told* him not to leave them down there in plain sight for somebody to sit on."

"Nobody sat on them, Ma," Harry told her. "What'd you do with them, Billy?"

Billy stopped petting the cat to look up. "What?"

"Dad's glasses. Where did you put them?"

Billy didn't answer, but Ariadne said, "I know where they are."

She got down from her seat at the breakfast table and picked up Alison's supply box from the side counter. Sure enough, when my sister opened the box, there were the missing glasses. Alison inhaled deeply before she spoke. "When you tell your father where they were, tell him *I* didn't put them there."

It didn't get the day off to a good start. And the herd of buffalo filling the road on our way into the park certainly didn't put Mr. Rupe into a better mood.

He had decided that today we were going to drive

north to the Mammoth Hot Springs. Hoping all the bad feelings had subsided, I said cautiously, "It sounds really interesting. It says the whole hillside is covered with a series of steps. The hot water comes up from the ground on the top, and then it flows down the steps, leaving mineral deposits as it comes over the edges. There are colored ponds on top of each layer, and the colors are caused by algae that depend on the temperature of the water."

Nobody said anything. Only my sister looked interested. Harry said, "I hope we finally see a bear today."

I liked the pools of blue and green water better than anything else we'd seen except for the animals. The pools began high up on the hillside. It was a stiff climb on the stairs and boardwalks to get to the top ones. I took pity on my sister. She couldn't hang on to both little kids at once and still have time to look at anything herself, so I kept Billy with me.

"Hang on to him tight," she warned, and I tried. Naturally Harry didn't think it was any responsibility of his to keep his little brother from being boiled alive in one of the deep blue pools.

In fact, the whole family took so little responsibility for the kids I wondered how they'd lasted this long.

Billy kept tugging on my hand to keep me moving. He wasn't much interested in the terraces or the multicolored algae. Harry was at least taking pictures of the colored pools and not complaining about not seeing a bear yet.

From the top we could see far below us, the parking lots and the strange tall rock formation called Liberty Cap that had once had hot water flowing out from its top. From here it looked like a giant anthill. There were tourists all over the place, some far enough away to look like ants moving up and down the trails. Halfway down the steep slope I saw Mrs. Rupe lighting another cigarette, sitting down to rest on a bench. She wasn't coming to the top. I didn't spot Mr. Rupe's bright yellow T-shirt anywhere.

"Hey," Harry said right beside me, "I felt the water running down over there and it's hot enough to cook eggs in, I bet."

I'd read more of the book about Yellowstone than he had. "The first explorers who found this place *did* cook in the hot springs," I said. "Look, are those elk tracks in between those two ponds?"

"And buffalo chips," Harry said. "If it's okay for the animals to walk out there, why are we restricted to the boardwalks?"

"Because it's dangerous," I said automatically. "And the animals can't read the signs. Maybe some of them fall in and get scalded to death."

I heard a splash and spun around to find Billy stretching out his arms as far as they could go, leaning over a pool with steaming water rippling over bright orange algae. "Did you throw something in the water?"

Billy tried to lean farther out over the forbidden territory, and I jerked him back. "Come on. We've climbed all the way to the top. It should be easier going down."

It wasn't, not much, but we finally did get to the bottom of the steps. Once we were away from the hot pools, Ariadne and Billy were allowed to run on ahead—on the assumption that drivers would take the responsibility for not running over them, apparently—and Alison and I fell behind the others.

"Did you notice, Lewis, when you looked down?" she asked quietly.

"Yeah," I agreed. "The blue car doesn't seem to be following us today. We could see it from the top if it were in any of the parking lots."

"Maybe," she said hopefully, "they've given up and gone home."

Fat chance, I thought, though I didn't say it.

I was more nervous about the blue car when I couldn't see it than when it was right behind us.

Chapter 10

I ought to have been able to enjoy seeing the wonders of Yellowstone more without those two guys dogging our heels, but it didn't work that way. Out of sight was definitely not out of mind.

I could see it was bothering Alison, too. She kept glancing behind us, checking out the parking areas, scanning the hordes of tourists that swarmed around us, and biting her lip a lot.

When we got back to the campground from the Mammoth Hot Springs, Harry and I were sent up to the store at the front of the campground to get a gallon of milk. I lost Harry when we went past the rig where Peggy was staying. I decided she must have several pairs of red shorts because we'd never seen her wear anything else.

Well, I could carry a gallon of milk by myself, I thought, and kept going. As the girl behind the counter gave me the change, she said, "Aren't you with the Rupe party, in the big motorhome?"

"Yeah," I admitted, hoping Mr. Rupe hadn't backed over somebody's kid or their dog.

"Did your friends find you okay?"

"Friends?" I echoed stupidly.

"The fellow who was asking about you this morning said he was supposed to meet you here. Your rig was gone so he was afraid you'd left, but I checked the reservations and told him you were booked for three more days, so you must have gone on into the park and you'd be back this evening."

"Uh . . . okay, thanks," I said, but the alarm bells were going off in my head.

As far as I knew, we weren't expecting any friends. And nobody had showed up since we returned to the campground. I mentioned it to Harry when I pried him away from Peggy.

"So what?" Harry asked.

"So who are the friends?"

"What difference does it make?"

"What if," I said patiently, "they're not *friends*?"

He frowned. "Meaning what? They're enemies? More than the ones we've already got, the ones who are chasing us all over Yellowstone?"

"Didn't you notice they *weren't* chasing us today? There wasn't a sign of them anywhere."

The wheels in his head were grinding slowly. "I didn't pay any attention. You think it was somebody trying to find out how long we'd be here?"

"Well, if they knew we weren't leaving for a while, there might not be so much reason to watch us every minute. Though I don't know how they think they're going to get at the motorhome, since we're either in it or it's locked in a parking area with so many people around they won't dare try to break in."

"Maybe they sent for another set of keys, and they're waiting for them to get here," Harry said. It was the smartest thing he'd come up with so far. "Let's walk past their rig again," he suggested, "and see what they're up to."

"Okay. You carry the milk the rest of the way," I told him, and swung the gallon jug at him.

The trailer and the car were where we had left them. The only thing that was different was that there was a flat tire on the Crown Victoria.

"That might explain why they didn't follow us today," I observed, and Harry nodded. "Nobody around now unless they're inside the trailer. Shall we look?"

"And have one of them looking back at us? I'll pass," I told him.

He called me a chicken, but he didn't go over by himself and look.

The next day we didn't see anything suspicious, nor any sign of the guys with the blue car. Nobody had fixed the tire—in the morning we checked before we left—and we couldn't tell if Syd and Ernie were in the trailer or not.

That morning we stopped at the museum in West

Yellowstone, the Montana town just outside the park. Harry had gotten more and more impatient because we hadn't seen any bears, and Ariadne kept saying the bears would bite.

"Hey, look!" I said when we entered the museum. "There's a bear, Ariadne! And he can't bite, because he's stuffed!"

The sign said his name was Old Snaggletooth. Ariadne had to be coaxed up close to him, but she finally got brave enough to reach out a finger and touch one of his great claws. Even I didn't feel like getting too close to his yellowed fangs.

We saw a video on the fire that swept through the park in 1988. It was pretty scary, but exciting. We had already seen a lot of the burned trees. My mom had been afraid it had ruined the park, but there had been regrowth since then, and they said that most of the animals had been able to outrun the flames.

None of the Rupes seemed interested in *why* the mud and the steam came rising out of the ground, but I thought it was fascinating. I couldn't help telling them some of what I'd read, whether they seemed interested or not.

That day we also spent a couple of hours at the Mud Volcano Trail. The trails were steep and it was hard work to climb them. Mrs. Rupe never did get all the way up to Sour Lake, and she hated the smells.

Nobody liked them, actually. They stunk of sulfur and other gases that came up through the water or the mud, from the volcanic heat far down inside the earth.

But it was worth the stink to see the Churning Caldron, and the Dragon's Mouth that seethed and rumbled so that Harry grinned as he looked into it. "Boy, if anybody fell into that thing, they'd never come up, would they? What a place to murder somebody, huh?"

I didn't think anybody with any brains would get close enough to get pushed in. Even if the mud or water wasn't boiling hot, it was likely to swallow anything up like quicksand.

Even Harry stopped to hear the information about Sulfur Caldron once I started reading it. "It's got the same sourness as battery acid or stomach fluids, it says."

"Yuk," Harry muttered as he peered into the slobbering mess.

Alison was holding the little kids' hands so hard that Ariadne complained. "Maybe," my sister suggested, "you could sit here on the bench with your mom while I go to the top." I knew she was really scared one of them would fall into one of these death traps, yet just as intrigued by them as I was.

"I'll stay with Mama, too. I'm tired," Billy said, and to our astonishment Mrs. Rupe didn't object, but let Alison leave them behind and go on up the climb with Harry and me. Mr. Rupe went off the main loop, I think, so he didn't have to listen to Harry and me talking.

I wondered why he'd brought his family on this trip, since he didn't actually seem to enjoy his kids very much.

We didn't miss him, though. The gang at home wouldn't believe all this stuff, I thought. Outsiders in the old days had ridiculed the men who discovered Yellowstone. Their tales of steaming springs and geysers and smelly pots of roiling mud in all kinds of different colors had sounded like hallucinations to those on the outside. It was kind of hard to believe even when you were actually looking at them.

When we went back to camp that afternoon and took a walk past Ernie and Syd's rig, the car and trailer were still there. So was a white paneled van that said LOCKSMITH on its side.

Several other kids were standing there watching, so Harry and I joined them. The locksmith was just finishing up.

"There you go," he said to Syd. "The new keys work just fine. You shouldn't have any more trouble."

They had new keys? Because their old ones were missing? I looked at Harry and he looked at me and licked his lips. I cleared my throat, keeping my voice low. "Weren't there keys in the car the first time we came over to check things out? It seems like I remember a key ring—that one with the Seahawks medallion on it."

Harry nodded. "Yeah. I saw it before Billy got in their car. I didn't notice when I dragged Billy out of the front seat."

"Did you see it *after* you pulled him out?"

Neither of us said any more, but we didn't need to. When we got back to the coach we cornered Billy in the bathroom where he was making pictures on the full-length mirror with a can of aerosol spray cleaner he'd found under the sink.

"What'd you do with the keys you stole out of that blue car?" Harry demanded.

We'd startled him, and Billy swung around with his thumb still on the spray device. White foam went all over both of us at thigh level, and Harry whacked the can out of his hand.

"Cripes! Pay attention to what you're doing," he said crossly, and grabbed a towel to wipe it off. "You aren't supposed to be playing with that."

"Nobody told me not to," Billy defended himself, which was probably true. Who could think of all the things to tell this kid not to do?

I didn't want the subject to be changed. "Where are the keys to that blue car?"

Billy stared at me, saying nothing.

Harry bent over and grabbed the front of his little brother's shirt. "We know you took the keys out of that car. So where did you put them? Get them for us."

"I can't," Billy said.

"Why not?"

And right that second I knew. "You threw them away, didn't you? Into one of those hot pools."

Harry straightened up, reading the same thing on Billy's face that I did. "Did you really? Holy cow!"

"Why?" I asked.

He hesitated, then said reasonably, "I wanted to see them disappear, the way the ice cubes did."

I exhaled. "So now we know why Ernie and Syd didn't keep following us. They must not have put the trailer keys on the ring with the car keys. They apparently have been staying in the trailer." I paused, then asked, "You didn't monkey with their tire, did you?"

He moistened his lips, and shook his head. "No. Charlie did that."

"Who's Charlie?" Harry and I asked together.

"The boy who has the little puffy white dog."

I knew the one he meant. Everybody in the campground who had dogs walked them every evening. I remembered Charlie, too. He was about ten, and on the chubby side.

"How come Charlie gave them a flat tire?" I asked.

"That man kicked his dog. It made Charlie mad, so when he came back he took that thing off his tire and it went *Sssss* and then it was flat."

Harry was staring at him. "How do you manage to learn all this stuff? We keep an eye on you all the time. You don't get to wander around loose."

A little smile curled Billy's lips. "Sometimes nobody watches for a few minutes."

"We were with him when he snitched the keys," I reminded Harry.

"Well, they'll fix their tire, and they've got new keys, so tomorrow they'll probably follow us again," Harry said.

They didn't, though. Maybe now that they knew we had reservations for a few more days, they didn't feel they had to, though what they were waiting for we didn't know. Maybe they really were waiting for another set of keys for our coach to arrive so they could use them anytime we were out looking at something in the park.

That morning we finally saw a bear.

It looked every bit as big as Old Snaggletooth at the museum. Harry howled and dived for his camera as the bear ambled out of the woods and began to cross the road ahead of us.

Mr. Rupe put on the brakes and pulled over to the side. Alison scooped up Ariadne and held her to the window, and I reached for Billy.

"Look! Look, it's a real bear!" I said.

Billy was on his knees on the couch, but the expression on his face didn't change. Ariadne's did; she was torn between being thrilled and being terrified, and Alison talked to her reassuringly.

Billy's eyes didn't even track as the bear padded across the road and paused to paw at something on the ground.

And finally it hit me.

I jerked off my glasses and held them over his eyes. "Can you see the bear now, Billy?"

Suddenly his face lit up in a big grin. "Wow!" he said.

Now I could barely make out the shape of the animal right ahead of us, and I realized why Billy was always swiping glasses, why he couldn't be bothered to look when we pointed out sights, why he preferred to do things right close up, like coloring or wrapping Scotch tape around the cat.

"He's so nearsighted he's practically blind to anything more than a few feet away," I said.

Nobody but Alison paid any attention. I'd tell them again, later, and I hoped they'd listen. Billy needed glasses with a prescription for nearsightedness. His father's were for the opposite, for seeing what was near, and that's why Billy hadn't been able to see with those.

From that time on, whenever we got where there was anything really worth seeing from Billy's viewpoint, I shared my glasses with him.

When we came upon a herd of buffalo, I held them on his nose so he could look, too. When the elk were grazing below us in a small meadow, he examined them through my lenses. When we came upon a small group of people watching a lone moose feeding along a small stream, and we were afraid he'd spook when Mr. Rupe got out and tried to get up close for a picture, I made sure Billy got to look for a few seconds before I did.

Mr. Rupe did get too close, and the moose decided to retreat. He was a very large animal, and I imagined what he could have done to the man if he hadn't chosen instead to trot off across the open area and into the woods.

One of the other tourists, a tall fleshy man with a

camera around his neck, too, scowled when Mr. Rupe came back to the road. "You chased him off while the rest of us were still taking pictures," he complained, loud enough for us to hear him from inside the coach.

"Don't blame it on me," Mr. Rupe said, "if you're too chicken to get close enough to get a good picture."

The man was red-faced and angry as we drove away. I looked at Harry, but I guess he was used to his dad being obnoxious. Mr. Rupe must have been considerate when he was working at the bank, but away from home he didn't seem to bother. I'd have been embarrassed to death if *my* dad had behaved that way.

Ten minutes later, when we stopped again because the road was full of buffalo and tourists with cameras or just gawking, Mr. Rupe went back to the bathroom. He came out looking furious.

"There's no water to flush the toilet! Who's been wasting water? We had half a tank when we left camp this morning, and now I can't even wash my hands, let alone flush!"

We all looked at Billy. He'd been intrigued by the pedal that flushed the toilet ever since the first time he got in the motorhome.

Harry reached over and pushed the button over the refrigerator that made the panel light up to monitor all the different systems. Instead of a green light indicating a safe level in our fresh water tank, there was a red one showing that the waste-water tank was full enough so it needed to be dumped.

Mr. Rupe growled something, stalked past us, and got back into the driver's seat. The culprit, Billy, sat on the floor petting William, ignoring the fuss.

When Mr. Rupe started up the coach, we lurched forward just as an impatient driver, annoyed that we had blocked the road for so long, tried to pass.

There was a grinding sound of metal on metal, and we were all thrown forward.

"Oh, Milton," Mrs. Rupe said, "you made Ariadne bump her head!"

Ariadne was crying. Alison tried to soothe her. Mrs. Rupe patted her knee.

Harry and I got out of the way when Mr. Rupe swore and turned off the engine, then headed for the door to talk to the irate driver who was getting out of his car.

We sat in silence while they exchanged insurance information. Whatever Mr. Rupe said to him, the other driver didn't seem to be pacified. Both of them were clearly angry.

Nobody said anything all the way back to the campground. Mr. and Mrs. Rupe announced that they were going with the Nabs, in their car, into West Yellowstone for the evening.

"You'll be perfectly all right by yourselves with all these people here," Mrs. Rupe said, as if all five of us kids were the responsibility of the strangers camped around us.

They had been gone about half an hour when we

heard the crackling sound of the PA system from the main office.

Harry looked up from the card game he and I were playing at the table. "What did they say?"

I leaned over and slid a window open so we could hear when it was repeated.

"Lone John is nearby. He is a buffalo bull who sometimes wanders away from the park to mingle with domesticated cattle on the nearby farms. He is wild, however, and can be dangerous if he's confronted. Stay in your rigs and don't approach him. Anyone in the pool house, laundry, or store, please stay there until we announce the all clear. Rangers are coming from Yellowstone to herd John back where he belongs."

It was almost dusk. We pressed our faces against various windows, trying to catch a glimpse of the runaway buffalo.

"There he is!" Harry said, and we all shifted to his window. I got a good look at him, coming along our road as if he belonged there, then handed my glasses to Billy. After all, I'd seen a lot of buffalo before he'd had any glasses to look through.

The voices from outside were perfectly clear because we still had a window open, and I recognized the speakers.

"It's a good thing that key was delivered today," Ernie said. "We're running out of time. If it hadn't come, I was going to bust out a window or something before they check out and go home."

"Well, this turned out great," Syd said. "They finally all left at the same time. Come on." And we heard the click of the key in the lock of the motor home.

Where we were, behind the tinted windows, it was practically dark. When the door swung open, I was scrabbling to get my glasses back from Billy.

"Uh-oh," I said, but there wasn't anything I could do to stop them from coming in. I was pretty sure none of the neighbors was paying any attention to us at all. They were still engrossed in Lone John.

Beside me, Harry faced the doorway, and his comment wasn't much more helpful than mine.

"Oh, crum," Harry said.

Chapter 11

Though it wasn't fully dark outside, it was dim inside the motorhome. We'd all been watching Lone John the buffalo wandering through camp, and had seen a van with the park rangers pull in. They were out of our sight, now, but nobody had turned the interior lights on yet when our door opened.

The men who'd been following us didn't see us immediately. Because of a radio playing in the trailer next door, they hadn't heard us, either.

"It's about time they left the rig unguarded," Ernie said as he came through the doorway, and it was clear he thought the coach was empty. "Let's move it. We gotta get this stash out of the country before the cops catch up to us."

Wc all froze. Harry and Billy and I were on the couch, Alison and Ariadne were in the copilot's seat, and nobody moved.

"They didn't leave the blinds closed," Syd said, pulling the door shut behind them. "We better do that before we turn on a light."

"Yeah. No sense attracting attention. With any luck these Rupes won't even know we were ever here. Open up that vent and grab the stuff and we'll hightail it out of this place."

Ernie took a step toward the front of the coach and tripped over Harry's feet. He went sprawling forward and landed across Billy and me and the cat, who was on Billy's lap.

For a few seconds our visitors seemed almost as scared as we were. William shot away from Billy, clawing and spitting. Judging by the swearing and the fact that the guy fell onto the floor, I figured the cat landed somewhere around his face.

Syd had fallen over Ernie before he realized anything was wrong, and Ariadne started screaming. It made the hair stand up on the back of my neck even though I knew she wasn't being murdered. Yet.

Syd recovered before his partner did. He scrambled to his feet. "Shut this kid up or she's in trouble!" he snapped. "Get those shades closed and a light on in here!"

A moment later we were blinking as he reached one of the wall lights. We all looked at each other as if we'd just seen ghosts, but Ariadne stopped screeching.

"Who are you?" she demanded, sitting up in Alison's lap.

There was some more swearing. Ernie was still breathing heavily as he surveyed us in disgust.

"I thought you said they were all gone, the rig was empty."

Syd gave us no more than a glance. "They're only kids. Let's get our stuff and get out of here."

"What do we do with *them*? Once they report to the cops, they'll have an APB out on us before we get out of the park."

I felt the cold run all the way through me. Even Harry wasn't wisecracking now. My tongue had gone dry and stuck to the roof of my mouth.

Syd grunted a nonanswer and bent over toward the front of the coach. He lifted the grating off the furnace vent in the floor, reaching down inside with one arm. Seconds later he straightened and said disbelievingly, "The stuff's not there."

"It's gotta be there," his partner said, equally incredulous. "Maybe it slid down deeper."

"No way it could have fallen any deeper. The pipe bends there." Syd straightened and looked straight at Harry. "Where is it?"

"What?" Harry asked, looking as much stupid as he did terrified.

"The bag that was in the vent. What did you do with it?"

Harry ran his tongue over pale lips. "I never saw any bag. I never touched anything."

Syd reached out and grabbed Harry's arm, jerking him to his feet. "Don't mess with me, kid. We want that bag."

Harry looked petrified. And innocent. Maybe

Billy knew where the bag was, if that was where he'd found the hundred-dollar bills, but the rest of us didn't know.

Billy had slid off the couch and worked his way past the open furnace vent to dig under the chair for William. He dragged him out and cuddled the indignant cat against him, crooning soothingly.

Ernie turned and grabbed me by the shoulder. I could tell he wasn't kidding; it hurt. "Where's the bag? Come on, don't play dumb! We want that money!"

"We don't have any money," I managed. "Honest. How would we know where you hid something?"

I didn't know how Billy found it, though I was sure he had. Maybe, even as nearsighted as he was, he'd been sitting on the floor and seen something through the grille. Anyway, he'd found it and then rehid it, I guessed. At that point I thought even Dad might have said to just hand over what they wanted, and called the cops later, but there was no way we could. I was afraid of what they'd do if they knew Billy had hidden it and wouldn't tell where.

Syd snarled an oath. "You kids sit down and stay put," he said, "while we look for it."

They didn't find it. They looked in the cupboards, and under the couch and the chairs, and in all the little nooks and crannies. Nothing.

"Maybe you got the wrong motorhome," Harry suggested as the man dumped papers and a package of cookies out of an overhead compartment.

"We don't have the wrong motorhome," Ernie

contradicted brusquely. "And you better hope we find it, wherever one of you hid it."

Billy looked up, the cat draped across his shoulder and against his face. "Are you going to shoot us?" he asked.

Ernie swore. Syd said, "Yeah, what are we going to do with them? They've seen us now. They can identify us."

Syd was the boss, the one who had tried to exchange coaches before we left home. I sure wished Mr. Rupe had let him do it.

Syd's face hardened. "We're getting out of here before the parents come back."

"Without the money?" Ernie asked in dismay.

"No, stupid, not without the money. It's got to be here somewhere. We'll just take the whole coach."

"Yeah," Harry said eagerly, sitting forward. "Take the whole coach! We'll just wait here for my folks!"

"And call the cops the minute we're gone? Not likely."

Five minutes later, as the motorhome eased out onto the highway heading north with Syd at the wheel, we knew the impossible was happening. We were being kidnapped.

"You kids get in the back and stay there," Ernie said, and we were glad to move as far away from the two of them as we could get.

Alison lifted the little kids onto the middle of the bed and the rest of us sat on the edges. After about a minute Harry reached up and turned on the speaker for the intercom, putting a finger over his lips to indicate to the rest of us that we were to be quiet. I'd noticed the control there, but we hadn't used it before. We hadn't been interested in what Mr. and Mrs. Rupe were saying up front, and they hadn't wanted to hear us.

Now we listened.

They didn't know we could hear them, so they talked freely. It didn't take us long to get the gist of the situation.

Ernie and Syd worked for the RV rental and repair business at legitimate jobs. But they had something else going on the side, evenings and on weekends.

Syd was a manager, and he had keys so he could get into the building when the rest of the staff wasn't around. We figured out that these two had been charging big amounts of money to "fix" things on motorhomes when they were brought in for regular maintenance or minor repairs.

Syd was an expert at making it look like there was a major problem, like an oil leak. Ernie would crawl under the rig and plant the oil both on the undercarriage and on the floor, so they could show it to the customer. They'd tell him if he didn't let them fix it, he could burn up his engine before he'd gone another twenty miles. Since lots of the people who drove the big rigs didn't know anything about them mechanically, they were conned into authorizing the repairs.

Syd's "repairs" weren't cheap. It sounded as if most "oil leaks" he "fixed" cost an unwary motorist anywhere from one to two thousand dollars, and it sounded as if he and Ernie did a lot of them. They also routinely charged for "new" parts they never installed.

It sounded to us, though, as if the owner of the business had begun to be a bit suspicious of them after he caught them working late at night. This made them nervous. Besides that, Syd had had an opportunity while the boss was on a business trip the previous week to steal the proceeds from several recent sales of new motorhomes. Since these big rigs were priced at two to three hundred thousand dollars apiece, and the buyers had written out checks in full payment, Syd as the manager was able to manipulate them into cash.

The trouble was, he knew that as soon as the boss came back, he was a dead duck. So he and Ernie had stashed their cash in the motorhome they intended to steal under the pretense of "renting" it for a vacation, planning to be out of the country before anyone missed the money or caught on to their larcenous dealings with unwary tourists.

Only all their plans had gone awry when a new employee had accidentally delivered "their" motorhome to the Rupes.

They'd been in a panic, controlled until now, thinking they could still pull it off. They only had another day before the boss would return, take one look at his books and deposit slips, and undoubtedly call in the police. Before that happened, they needed to be across the border into Canada.

They couldn't go without the cash they'd hidden

in the motorhome, and they sounded desperate to get their hands on it.

They were convinced someone, probably Mr. Rupe, had found the bag and intended to keep it rather than turn it in to the authorities.

They seemed positive that the money had been removed from *their* hiding place and rehidden somewhere else. And, miraculously, they seemed to believe us when we said we didn't know where that was.

But they hadn't expected to find kids in the motorhome, didn't realize we had known they were following and watching us, nor that we were now listening to their conversation. Ariadne put her thumb in her mouth and fell asleep, but twice Harry slapped a hand over Billy's mouth when he started to talk. "Shhh! Be quiet so they don't hear us!" he whispered.

They had started to argue about what to do with us.

"It'll take us close to ten hours to reach the Canadian border and cross into Alberta. We can't try to take those brats through the inspection; they'd give us away for sure," Ernie said.

They seemed to be assuming that once they got into Canada, they'd be safe. The Canadians wouldn't arrest them for crimes committed in the United States, not for theft. But they might be cooperative with the American authorities if the two were caught kidnapping a bunch of kids. That was a federal crime, one the Canadian authorities might agree to extradite them for.

They didn't want to take us along, but they didn't

know what to do with us. They couldn't leave us where we'd report them to the police, because the cops wouldn't even have to chase them. They'd just call ahead to the border patrol and stop them there.

It was clear they were thinking they'd have to get rid of us before we went much farther.

We only had one little light on in the bedroom, but we could see each other's scared faces. Billy, cuddling the cat against his face, was dozing off like Ariadne. At least *they* weren't terrified. Harry and Alison and I stared at each other, petrified.

"Are they going to kill us?" my sister mouthed.

"I don't think they've got any guns to shoot us with," Harry murmured, his back to the microphone set into the wall so it wouldn't pick up his voice.

The two up front were still talking, so I guessed it was safe to talk if we did it very softly. "There are other ways to kill somebody," I said. "But they could be extradited from Canada for murder and kidnapping, especially of kids. I don't think they'll kill us."

"Nah," Harry agreed. "Their chances of getting away with it are too small, even if they leave the United States."

The three of us sat there in the dim light, wishing we could believe what we'd just said.

"You can't just move to Canada because you want to," I muttered. "You have to have papers and everything to emigrate from the U.S. to Canada. Our uncle did it, and he had to have a physical exam and show how he'd make a living up there and fill out a whole bunch of forms. So just because they cross the border doesn't mean they're home free."

"This is a pretty big and classy looking motorhome," Harry contributed. "It must be four or five hundred miles to the border, and this rig draws a lot of attention. There aren't very many like it on the highways. You think when my dad finds out we're all gone he isn't going to describe it to the cops? That nobody's going to spot it before they get anywhere near Alberta?"

"Surely," Alison said tensely, "nobody's crazy enough to kill five kids for *money*."

There was a moment's silence as the big motorhome thrummed through the night. It was as if it knew there was someone other than Mr. Rupe driving. It had never sounded so powerful and so fast.

How long would the Rupes and the Nabs stay in town? How fast could they organize police pursuit when they got back to camp and found we and the motorhome were missing?

Up front Syd swore.

We froze, listening.

"What's the matter now?" Ernie asked.

"We're practically out of fuel. Wouldn't you think that idiot of a Rupe would refuel before he stopped for the night? Look at that!"

Harry squirmed around on the edge of the bed. "They'll have to stop before long. Dad was going to fill up in West Yellowstone first thing in the morning. Maybe we'll have a chance to get help."

I wondered if his heart was hammering as hard as mine was.

Syd's voice crackled a little, coming through the intercom. "Ernie, start tearing this place apart. Find that bag. Once we have it, we don't have to stick with this outfit. And there's nothing that says we have to leave these brats where anybody can find them right away. Once we cross into Alberta, it won't matter what they tell anybody."

I saw Alison swallow. Sure, that was probably their best bet. To dump us and the motorhome in some place where we couldn't walk out in less than a few days, and wouldn't be spotted in the meantime.

There were plenty of such places in Montana. Not to mention some spots where they could send us over a cliff or into a river where we might *never* be found.

"I guess they wouldn't hang up at stealing another car or two once they dump this," Harry muttered, leaning close to me. "What we gonna do, Lewis?"

I could see the same question on my sister's face. "Maybe they'll find their money and just leave us somewhere," I muttered.

But they didn't find the bag of cash. Ernie dumped things out of cupboards, pulled out drawers, looked among the frozen foods in the freezer, and emptied the ice maker into the sink. We could watch him in the small mirror over the credenza at the side of the aisle.

Then he came back and pawed around in the medicine cabinet and through the towels in the cabinet under the sink. When he finally turned toward the bedroom, we all sort of shrank out of his way while he pulled the drawers out of the nightstands and moved things around in the closet. Then he told us to get off the bed so he could look under the pillows and the mattress.

"The little kids are asleep," Alison protested, but when Ernie growled deep in his throat, she picked up Ariadne without waking her, and Harry did the same with Billy, backing into the bathroom to get out of the way.

There was nothing under the bedding. There was nothing in the laundry hamper. There was nowhere else to look.

Ernie stalked back up front, fury in every line of his body. "It's not here, Syd. They must have moved it out of the coach."

"Why would they do that?" Syd snapped. I was glad he hadn't talked while Ernie was back with us or they'd have realized there was an intercom on and that we could hear them talking. "It's too big to stick in the guy's pocket and carry to town with him. It's gotta be here somewhere."

Alison eased Ariadne back onto the bed, then got out of Harry's way so he could do the same with Billy. The cat slid out of Billy's limp arms and dropped to the floor.

I raised a blind to look out at the night, where it was full dark now.

"I don't know where we are, but it doesn't look as

if they're going into West Yellowstone to refuel," I said. Only a few lights showed as we passed scattered houses.

"If they don't refuel, they won't get very far. This rig only gets six miles to the gallon, and the tank was practically on empty," Harry said, peering over my shoulder.

I thought the way Mr. Rupe drove it would have been a miracle if we'd got *four* miles to the gallon, but I didn't say it. Right that minute I'd have been happy to have him running over small trees and nudging other vehicles.

Behind us, Ariadne stirred and sat up. "I'm hungry," she said.

"Oh, honey, I can't get you anything to eat now," Alison told her. "How would you like to . . . to color some pictures?"

Ariadne scowled. "I don't want to color. I want a sandwich."

"There are some nasty men up front, so we can't get at the food," Alison said earnestly. "And we must speak very softly, so they don't hear us. Look, my supply box is here. That man knocked it on the floor and I picked it up. Here, would you like the blue crayon?"

To my surprise, Ariadne accepted the crayon and a magazine to put under her sheet of paper. "I'll draw a bear," she offered.

"What'll we do when we stop at a service station?" Harry asked, still looking out into blackness. "Yell for help?"

I hardly heard him. I was watching my sister. She had laid out four sheets of paper together and was printing on them with a black marker. I read the printing upside down. "Help, we're being kidnapped," I read aloud. "How's anybody going to see them in the dark, doing sixty miles an hour?"

"We'll have to stop pretty soon," Alison said, "and this might be safer than trying to call for help when those men will certainly try to stop us. What am I going to use to stick them on the windows? Billy used up all the Scotch tape."

"Band-Aids," I said, and got some from the medicine cabinet. What the heck, it couldn't hurt anything to stick the signs on the windows on both sides of the coach, but I didn't really think they were going to save us.

"Let's write 'This is a stolen vehicle,'" I suggested, handing Harry a piece of paper and a crayon.

"Uh," Harry said uncertainly, "how do you spell *vehicle*?"

Once the signs were in place, with the shades closed over them, our captors wouldn't notice them if they came back here.

By this time Billy woke up again, and coaxed the cat back up onto the bed. He didn't seem to be interested in anything that happened much over a couple of feet from him, which I guess was natural if he couldn't see beyond that.

He looked up at me, now, though, and asked, "Are they going to kill us?"

He didn't sound very concerned. I wondered if he thought killing was like on TV cartoons, where a character got squashed flat in one episode and was miraculously recovered in the next one.

I wished I could think this was like a cartoon episode, that it wasn't really dangerous, and that we'd come out okay tomorrow.

The kidnappers were all too real, though, and things hadn't worked out the way Ernie and Syd had planned. When they couldn't get Mr. Rupe to trade motorhomes, they thought it would be easy to follow us and slip into this one when nobody was looking and retrieve their loot. Only that hadn't worked, and then we'd surprised them as much as they'd surprised us when they'd gotten hold of the door key. They were in a bad mood.

They couldn't afford to let us stick around to identify them.

"I wonder how much money they hid," Harry said, slumping onto the edge of the bed beside Billy. "I'd like to know how much my life is worth."

"A lot," Billy said.

I stared at him. I didn't think he'd meant that Harry's life was worth a lot. "How much money, Billy?" I asked.

He looked confused. I decided he'd spoken without thinking and was now reluctant to go on with that line of thought. He buried his face in William's fur.

I was totally convinced that Billy was the one who had moved that money. And I knew I didn't want to hand it over to the thieves unless that was the only way to save our lives. Well, I couldn't hand over anything I couldn't find.

"We've got to make our move when we stop for fuel," I said. Escaping was our first priority. After we were safe, we'd coax the information out of Billy. "That's probably the only chance we'll get. While we're moving we haven't got a hope of escaping, or even anyone noticing us in the dark."

"So what's our move?" Harry asked eagerly. "You have a plan, Lewis?"

I wished I did. "Nothing foolproof," I had to admit. "But we put up signs on the windows, and we need to do anything we can to attract attention when we stop. Maybe there'll be other customers, but at least there'll be an attendant pumping gas." I sure hoped there would, that it wouldn't be a self-service place with no one on duty who'd come anywhere near us.

"Maybe we could climb out the windows," Harry said thoughtfully. "We could get one of them open and be ready to run the minute we stop."

"Without them catching us?" Alison asked. "If we could lock a door between us it might work, but they'd stop us before more than one or two of us made it. And it's a long way to the ground, especially for the little kids. Nobody could even reach up high enough to lift them down."

"Maybe we wouldn't all have to escape through a window," I said. "Maybe if one of us got out and ran for a phone the police would come and save everybody else."

Harry was chewing on his lip. "If only we had a weapon of some kind to slow them down if they came after us. But short of grabbing a butcher knife, there's no kind of weapon."

"They're not going to let us walk out in the other room and get a knife," Alison said. "And they're so much bigger and stronger, they'd take it away before we could do anything with it."

We hadn't looked at Billy for a few minutes, and all of a sudden the cat bolted away from him and fled to hide in the bathroom. I caught a glimpse of William and only realized what was peculiar when I saw what Billy was holding.

"Did you squeeze all that toothpaste out onto the cat?" I demanded, taking the tube away from him.

"He likes it," Billy said, smiling.

"No, he doesn't like it. Now what are people going to use to brush their teeth?"

Billy smiled wider and shrugged.

I wasn't sure where he'd found the toothpaste—probably Ernie had thrown it out of a cupboard when he was searching—but I went to put it into the medicine cabinet, which was too high up for Billy to reach.

And I stopped with the door wide open as the idea hit me.

"Hey, maybe we do have a weapon or two," I said, just as Alison spoke excitedly from behind me.

"Lewis! There's a police car passing us! Maybe they'll see our signs!"

Chapter 12

I got to the window in time to see the police cruiser sail right on by us. Nobody saw our signs calling for help.

Alison bit her lip. Harry said the kind of word my mom would chew me out for using.

"I keep looking at that CB up front," Harry said in frustration, "but I don't know how to use it."

"I know how to use it," I told him, "but there's no way they're going to let us get close enough to do it. But I thought of something else. It may not be as effective as a gun against these guys, but it might help slow them down enough so at least one of us can get away to call for help when we stop."

Right that minute we felt the coach slowing down, and within seconds we were turning off the highway. We made enough space between the slats of the blinds to see that we were pulling into a service station, which meant we only had seconds to get ready. I explained quickly.

Our ammunition wasn't great, but it was the best we could manage. While Harry struggled to get one of the big side windows open—there was no window in the back because it was covered with a closet—I jerked the tops off the cans I found in the medicine cabinet.

"Who's going out the window?" Harry asked, jerking on the cord to make sure the shade stayed up. "You want me to do it?"

"Lewis is a fast runner," Alison said. "Let him go. Don't sprain an ankle when you land, Lewis."

"I'll try not to." My heart was pounding as we rolled slowly into the lighted area. There was only one other car at the pumps, an old pickup with two big shaggy dogs in the back of it. "Anybody see a phone?"

We had the shades on both sides out of the way, now, but we couldn't get the second window open. It was stuck. So I knew which one I had to get out of, and it was on the same side as the door up front, so when one of our captors got out he'd see me immediately.

The station building itself was lit up, and there had to be a telephone in there, I thought. So if I didn't spot one anywhere else, I'd make a dash for that open door. As far as I could tell, there was only one man on duty, talking to the driver from the old pickup alongside of us. Like the building, they were on the far side of the lot from us.

From the front of the coach Syd yelled, "You kids stay put and keep quiet and you won't get hurt!"

"Yeah, sure," Harry muttered. And then, to me, "Go for it, Lewis!"

A yell from up front told me I'd been spotted bailing out. I landed on the balls of my feet, no sprained ankle, and headed for the back of the motorhome.

I heard Ernie come out the front door, feet pounding on the pavement behind me, and I felt as if his hot breath was on the back of my neck.

I didn't see what happened then, just heard about it later. At the moment I expected a big hand to grab the neck of my shirt and jerk me off my feet, Harry leaned out the window with a full can of shaving cream and sprayed it directly into Ernie's eyes.

I didn't know why Ernie was yelling and swearing, but the dogs in the old pickup started barking ferociously at this activity only a few yards from them. I was running for the station, where the two men in the lighted area turned to see what all the commotion was.

Inside the coach, Syd headed for the bedroom to see what was going on. Alison hit him in the face with hair spray, and while he was practically blinded and bent over, she clobbered him on the head with the heavy-duty flashlight Mr. Rupe had kept beside the bed. It didn't do any serious damage, but by the time he'd recovered enough to lift his head, she'd shaken up the hair spray again for another burst.

I heard the ruckus behind me and ran for all I was worth, hoping none of the kids was getting hurt. Ariadne was screaming as if she was being killed, but Ariadne could screech that way just in excitement.

"What the heck's going on?" the service man asked, coming toward me wiping his hands on a rag. The pickup driver was right after him, alarmed about his dogs.

"Don't nobody hurt my dogs!" he yelled. "Rags! Jumper! Come 'ere!"

"The cops!" I gasped, nearly going to my knees in front of them. "Call the cops!"

They were close enough now to read our signs. The pickup man, whose dogs (according to Harry, later) had literally run over Ernie and knocked him flat as they leaped out of the truck bed, gaped at the signs. "Kidnapped?" he said. "This ain't a joke? That rig's been stolen?" His dogs were leaping up on him and only subsided when he commanded them to sit.

"Call the cops before they drive away!" I begged. "There are four more kids in there!"

I didn't know yet that Ernie and Syd were in no shape to drive away. Between the shaving cream and the hair spray, neither of them could see very well for a few minutes.

And then I spotted the greatest sight of my life. A police cruiser pulled onto the lot and cut across in front of the motorhome.

A very tall, very sturdy looking police officer got out and sauntered over to look closely at the signs in our rear windows. Then he turned toward the three of us standing there in the open.

He sort of rested one hand on the gun he had holstered on his hip, casual-like. "Any of you belong with the motorhome?" he asked.

I was getting my breath back. "Yes, sir. The two men driving it stole it, back at the campground outside of Yellowstone. My sister and three other kids are trapped in there. These guys stole a lot of money and hid it in there, in a furnace vent. It's gone, and they can't find it, which is why they stole the coach. But I think Billy probably knows where the money is."

I'd run out of breath again by that time. The officer was looking at me, evaluating what I was saying, and I suddenly got really nervous. What if he decided I was just some smart aleck trying to play a joke on him? I was afraid I'd sounded like one.

He lifted off his uniform cap and scratched his head. "Hmm."

About then Ernie came around the front of the coach. He'd wiped off most of the shaving lotion, and his eyes were red and irritated-looking. He acted like he didn't even see the cop or the other two men, and glared at me.

"I told you not to get out of the motorhome," he said. "I got a notion to lick you good."

He finally looked at the cop. "He done something, officer? This boy, he don't always mind me the way he ought to."

"He's not my dad," I said quickly. "Check his ID. He's from an outfit that rents RVs, back in Marysville, Washington. He can't prove he rented this motorhome, because it was rented to Mr. Rupe. Three of the kids with us are Rupe kids; the other one's my sister. Don't let him drive away with us."

The officer hardly acted like he heard me, but he said to Ernie, "Could I see your driver's license, sir?"

"Uh, it's in the coach. I need to fuel up," Ernie said to the attendant. "Maybe you can do that while I get the papers the officer needs. I'll be right back, sir."

But the cop didn't wait where he was; he went along, and stood in the doorway while Ernie looked for papers, or pretended to. Syd was at the kitchen sink, washing his eyes out under the faucet. I'd heard hair spray could knock flies and other insects out of the air if you hit them with it, and even kill them. I hoped Syd's eyes were stinging like crazy, so he'd have to behave.

Spray cans weren't the ideal weapons, but they'd helped a lot. If Harry hadn't slowed Ernie down with shaving cream, I might never have gotten away from the motorhome to let anybody know we were in trouble.

Ernie came back with some papers. "To tell you the truth, officer, my eyes are bothering me so much I can't tell for sure what I got. I think these are the rental papers, just like the boy said. Made out to Milton Rupe. I seem to have mislaid my wallet, but it's here somewhere. Soon as my eyes quit hurting I'll find it for you."

The officer appraised his watering eyes, and then glanced toward the man at the sink.

"I'll have to ask everybody to step out of the vehicle," he said. "Including whoever's in the rear."

"That's only my kids," Ernie said. "They been put to bed. No need to wake them up, is there?"

"They're not his kids," I said quickly. "He kidnapped all of us."

"Out of the coach, please," the officer said, stepping aside to clear the doorway. "Everyone. Including the children."

They tried to bluff long enough to get away, but the cop wasn't buying their story. It wasn't until a backup unit had arrived that we found out the first cop was the one who had passed us earlier. He *had* seen our signs, and at first he'd thought it was a hoax. When he thought about it, though, he decided he'd better check it out.

Boy, were we glad he did.

As they made our kidnappers get into the back of one of the police cars, Syd looked at me and said, "Okay, I give up. What did you do with it?"

I didn't answer.

While we were waiting in the motorhome for one of the officers to get Mr. and Mrs. Rupe, though, I went over and over in my head all the places everybody had already looked for the money without finding it. There *had* to be at least one place they hadn't looked, I thought.

The little kids got hungry, and Harry got out another big bag of chips and divided them up on paper plates. "I want a candy bar," Billy said, and he went to the refrigerator and got one out of one of the crispers at the bottom. Mrs. Rupe had stored one of them completely full of Snickers and Hershey bars and peanut butter cups. She hadn't brought any fruit to put in that one, only a little bit of salad stuff in the second bin. She hadn't really cooked a meal since we'd left home, so most of it had rotted, untouched.

And that's when the idea hit me. "Billy," I said, "is the money in the refrigerator?"

He stared at me and said, "It's mine. Finders keepers."

"They looked in the refrigerator," Alison said.

They had, but I had a hunch. I pulled out the second crisper, and poked through the wilted lettuce, a cucumber that had gone soft and squishy, and a few tomatoes with yucky spots on them. All the stuff for the salads we never got to eat.

And there it was, under the rotting vegetables. The bag was wrapped in a piece of crumpled foil—how had Billy been clever enough to think of that, or was it just a fluke that he'd hidden it so it looked like leftover lunch meat or something?

Billy started to cry when I pulled it out and unwrapped it. "It's mine," he said, but I think he already knew it wasn't.

We thought the Rupes were pretty casual about their kids, but when they got back to the campground and found the motorhome and all of us gone, they came unglued.

Mr. Rupe might be arrogant and sometimes rude to strangers, but he was used to giving orders and having them obeyed. He had the county sheriff's department and the state patrol in high gear within minutes.

Other units were already looking for us by the time our patrolmen called in to say they'd found us, so we'd have been rescued before long even if we hadn't stuck the signs on the windows and even if I hadn't leaped out a window to get help. But everybody thought we'd been very brave and clever; even Mr. Rupe nodded approval of our pressurized can weapons.

Mrs. Rupe praised us while she hugged Billy and Ariadne; she was really impressed with our responsible reactions to the situation. I figured Alison had a lifetime job as a sitter if she wanted it.

Harry and I took turns explaining the scam Syd and Ernie had been involved in, and I was glad we'd found the money to back it up, because it sounded pretty wild. Billy kept insisting that he'd found the cash and it should be his, but his father gave him a long look.

"Don't be silly, son. It's stolen money. It has to go back to the people it belongs to . . . after the police have held it for evidence in the trial when they send the two of them to jail for a long time."

"But you always said 'finders keepers,'" Billy protested tearfully.

"Not with thousands of other people's dollars," Mr. Rupe said firmly, putting an end to the discussion.

Billy finally stopped fussing about it when they promised him that as soon as we got home, they'd get him some glasses like mine so he could see what was going on around him.

The less said about our trip home the better.

As Mr. Rupe turned into the driveway, Mrs. Rupe exclaimed, "Watch it, Milton, you're going to hit the—"

The motorhome clipped the garbage cans and they fell over, clattering, and rolled into the gutter.

Mr. Rupe turned off the ignition and sighed. "I think I'll stick to driving something smaller than this from now on. It's made me a nervous wreck, and I didn't think I had a raw nerve in my body," he said.

We'd made enough noise so my folks came out and were waiting to meet us as we got out of the coach.

Billy bailed out first and ran to meet them. "I'm going to get glasses just like the ones Lewis has," he said. "I'm sorry I broke *his* glasses. I didn't mean to sit on them."

The welcoming smile on Mom's face flickered uncertainly. "Lewis?" she asked, stepping forward to see me more clearly. The lens hadn't fallen out, but there was a crack in the middle of it that divided her face into two parts.

"Hi, Mom," Alison said, reaching for a hug. "I need to hang out my sleeping bag to dry right away. It was under one of the skylights that was broken when we came through the storm near Missoula, and it got soaked. I saved one of the hailstones that fell through, in the freezer. It's as big as an egg."

"I spit in the Grand Canyon of the Yellowstone," Billy said proudly, struggling to control William, who was trying to escape. "It went all the way to the bottom."

"You're home a day earlier than we expected," Mom said, no longer smiling but anxious. "Did you have trouble?"

Mr. Rupe was opening up the lower level bays to unload. "Oh, it worked out all right," he said. "But after everything that happened we decided we'd had enough of sightseeing. We just wanted to come home. The kidnappers are in jail in Montana, and Lewis found the money."

"Billy felt sure the money would be his, since he found it first," Mrs. Rupe said, allowing her cigarette ashes to drift all around her as she waved a hand. "But of course that was out of the question. I'm so tired, I can't possibly cook. Let's call out for pizza, maybe fried chicken."

"Kidnappers?" Mom echoed faintly.

"Money?" Dad repeated, scowling.

"When Billy cried, though, the people at the campground said he could keep William," Harry reported, as my parents looked more confused by the moment. "Some camper had left him behind there in the first place."

"I have to go potty," Ariadne said.

"Uh, I have dinner on the stove," Mom said, looking as if she'd been hit by a hurricane. "Come on inside, kids. We'll talk about all this later. Thank you so much for taking Alison and Lewis with you, Mrs. Rupe. I'm sure they had a . . . wonderful time."

"If you have any questions after Lewis tells you the story, I'll be glad to fill in the details," Mr. Rupe told Dad as he emptied the first compartment.

When we got in the house, Mom checked the stuff on the stove and said, "You obviously have a lot to tell us." She glanced sideways at Alison who was putting another two place settings on the table. "Did the Rupes offer you money for caring for the children?"

"No," Alison said cheerfully, "but I survived the trip, and I sure learned a lot about baby-sitting. I should qualify as an expert from now on."

"I had fried chicken and all the fixings planned for your homecoming dinner," Mom said. "I didn't expect you tonight, so I don't have any of your favorites."

"Meat loaf is good, Mom. Smells great," I said as we took our places. I took a big helping of salad, and then another big one of green beans, loading up my plate.

"Tell us," Dad commanded, unwilling to wait any longer. "Start with the kidnappers."

Mom was still trying not to be upset, trying to make things seem ordinary. "And your glasses, Lewis. How did Billy manage to sit on them? Why weren't you wearing them?"

"We were sharing them, and we'd come past the last of the buffalo so Billy wanted to see them. He's as blind as I am without glasses."

"Who was kidnapped?" Dad asked in a tone that meant he wasn't going to be sidetracked another moment.

So between us Alison and I told them the whole story. Well, almost. Neither of us mentioned Mr. Rupe's terrible driving. It didn't matter because we never intended to get into a car with him again. We'd figured out that a person could be intelligent and responsible in other ways and still not be a very competent driver.

Mom looked at me kind of funny when I took a second helping of green beans (when I was little I used to feed them to the dog under the table when nobody was looking) while Alison told them about the hail. It had not only broken our skylights but had made the freeway so icy that all traffic had stopped for nearly half an hour, and then when we got to the campground it had cooled off the heated pool enough so Ariadne complained about how cold it was. "It was so loud on the roof that we had to yell to hear each other," Alison concluded.

Dad had a look on his face that made me think he suspected he hadn't yet heard the whole story. "But Yellowstone was terrific," I said. "I hope our whole family can go back together someday. You'd like the animals, and the paint pots, and the geysers, and the mud volcanoes, Mom."

She was looking at me strangely, too. Not only surprised that we were home early, and I was eating salad and green beans, but as if I'd changed in some way she couldn't quite pin down. "I didn't make any dessert for tonight," she said. "I was planning on brownies for tomorrow."

"That's okay. We don't need any dessert." I didn't tell her that instead of stopping to eat lunch on the way home we'd finished off the junk food we were carrying, including two or three candy bars apiece. The thought of any more sugar at the moment made me a little bit queasy. "I'll rest up for brownies tomorrow. It was a great trip, but I'm sure glad to be home."

"Me, too," Alison said.

When the phone rang, she got up to answer it, and I listened to her saying, "Oh, hello, yes, this is Alison. Oh, she did? How nice of her. Yes, I've had considerable experience baby-sitting for young children. Certainly, Mrs. Potter, I'd be glad to stay with your children tomorrow night. Yes, thank you. See you then."

I'd thought she was all burned out by Ariadne and Billy, but she hung up with a grin. "That new neighbor of the Mahoneys has two little girls. She's asked me to sit, and if the kids like me it'll be every Thursday night while they go bowling and then other times once in a while."

"I thought you'd be tired of baby-sitting after this trip," Mom said. "How were the Rupe kids?"

I thought of Ariadne at the top of the cedar tree, and wetting the bed, and with ice cream dripping off both elbows. I remembered Billy Scotch-taping the cat, and hiding my glasses, and tying Alison's shoelaces together.

"Okay," Alison said, and I echoed, "Okay."

Willo Davis Roberts

As always, the first paper I had to write when school started was on how I spent my vacation. I told the truth, every word, and there was a big red A at the top of the paper when Mrs. Garvey handed it back to me.

She was smiling. "My, Lewis, you certainly have a wonderful imagination," she said.